Flowers in the Snow

Book One of The Edenville Series

Danielle Stewart

Copyright Page

An *Original* work of Danielle Stewart.
Flowers in the Snow Copyright 2015 by Danielle Stewart

ISBN-13: 978-1507700877

ISBN-10: 1507700873

Cover Art by: Ginny Gallagher
Website: www.Ginsbooknotes.com

Dedication

To those who open their hearts and their doors to the children who need love. You are changing the world.

Prologue

<u>Betty</u>

It's funny, even when you know something's coming, it can still take you by surprise. I've known for months this letter would arrive, but I still can't bring myself to open it. Peeling back the glued flap of the familiar pink envelope feels like pulling the lever of a floodgate that will set free the tears I've been holding in.

Instead I just step onto my porch, hold it to my heart as I settle into my rocking chair. The sun is on its way down now, and as it paints the sky in all manner of reds and pinks, I listen to the gaggle of people moving around my kitchen. What a family I've built over these last ten years. I have more kids to my name than I ever imagined, and their kids all call me Grammy, yet almost none of them are my blood. That's the lesson of my life; family is who you decide to love, not necessarily who you're related to.

Another lesson of my life: you can get a second chance at love even when the first one was perfect in its own way. Burying my husband years ago, after he was killed in the line of duty, nearly broke me. But my daughter, Jules, and I have rebuilt what was destroyed, and with my second husband, Clay, I've found a way to go on. He's made my dreams of owning a restaurant a reality. It doesn't mean I've forgotten about Stan; it simply means I love him enough to move on with my life.

Today as I sit on my porch I am everything I ever wanted to be. Not many people can say that, so I know I'm lucky. But that isn't enough to stave off the sorrow that comes with knowing one of the people who has been a stepping-stone on my path to happiness has taken her last breath. She's lost her battle with cancer, and the letter I'm holding will be the last I ever receive from her. For over forty years I've frequently reached into my mailbox and found a pink paisley envelope with my friend's familiar scrawl. In all that time we never ran out of things to tell each other. We never ran out of kind words. We never ran out of love for each other. I always knew death would be the only thing to break the bond we had. I just hoped there would have been a couple more decades before we had to say goodbye.

A burst of laughter spills out the open windows, and I can't help but smile at the joy contained within these walls. Each adult inside my house came with his or her own baggage. Truckloads of it, really. Some abused, some deserted, some confused, and some afraid, but they all turned up here, needing one thing. Love. I am the flame and they are the moths. Some people may call that a curse, but for me it's been a blessing.

I'd like to take credit for the way my heart and home are open to everyone I meet, but I know I wasn't born that way. Love is taught. It's handed down. And I was lucky enough to have someone take the time to show me how to really love. Not just say the words, but love with my whole self, so even when I'm not with her—she can feel me there.

Chapter One

"Are you all right, Grammy?" Frankie asked as she settled into Betty's lap and wrapped her arms around her neck. She was too big to sit there comfortably, but there was no way in hell Betty would ever refuse a chance to hold her oldest granddaughter. Experience told her these hugging days were fleeting, so she'd better soak up every hug she could before they were gone.

"I'm just sitting here thinking of years gone by. It's been a long life, baby, but it has also gone so fast I can't stand it. The days are long, but the years—oh goodness, the years have just melted away."

"You've got a lot of years left, Grammy. Remember you have to help me pick a boyfriend in a few years. That's our deal," Frankie teased as she flashed a playful smile.

Betty laughed and affectionately tucked Frankie's red hair behind her ear. "*You* said a few years, I said ten years. And girl, I can tell you now there won't be a boy on this earth I think is good enough for you." Planting a kiss on the crown of Frankie's head, Betty pulled the envelope away from her chest and held it where the child could see.

"What's that?" Frankie asked, crinkling up her freckle-covered nose.

"It's a letter from a friend. The last letter she'll ever send me. I'm afraid to open it," Betty admitted, knowing she was starting a conversation she wouldn't be able to easily stop.

3

"You're not afraid of anything, Grammy. You're the bravest person I know," Frankie said earnestly as she batted her long lashes over her crystal blue eyes.

"I haven't always been. I was your age once, and I was plenty scared. As a matter of fact I wasn't much older than you when I met this friend. She changed my life."

"How do you know it's the last letter she'll send you? Are you fighting?" Frankie cocked her head sideways to get a better look at the envelope as though she'd be able to see something on it that would give her a clue.

"No girl, we aren't fighting. The only fighting we've ever done has been on the same side of a war. She's gone on to heaven now. Unfortunately there's no way to mail something from up there, no matter how badly we wish we could," Betty said with a sniffle.

"I'm sorry, Grammy." Frankie sighed as she rested her head on Betty's shoulder.

With a quake, Betty began to shudder, unable hold back the tears rolling down her cheeks.

"Are you crying, Grammy?" Frankie asked in shock, witnessing something she'd never seen before. "Mom, Mommy, something's wrong with Grammy," she shouted through the open window.

A thundering herd of feet came charging through the screen door. Adults and children alike gathered around Betty, who was now sobbing with no shame for it. "I'll be all right in a minute," she choked out, but it didn't seem to convince anyone.

"What is it, Ma?" Jules asked, dropping to her knees and holding her mother's hand in hers.

Over Jules's shoulder Betty could see everyone moving in closer. Bobby and Piper each held a twin in their arms and looked on with thick worry. Many years ago, Bobby had started out as the neighbor's boy who needed a place to go when his parents couldn't keep it together. He was the first to feel healed by Betty's cooking and warmed by her love. Through him she met the rest of them. Piper, his wife, was the worst off of them all—the most damaged by a childhood gone wrong. Betty would never admit to any of them, but there were days, through the worst of her times, she wasn't sure Piper would make it. But now, looking at the grown woman she'd become, there was no doubt left in her mind; Piper had made it.

"They are beautiful babies," Betty hummed, reaching out her hand and touching Piper's daughter, Sky, gently on the leg. "I can't believe they'll be in kindergarten this year. You've made a wonderful family, and every time I look at them it reminds me of the biggest truth in this world. Love is greater than any differences we have."

Bobby and Piper hadn't thought twice when they got the call telling them they were matched with a set of twins who needed an immediate placement. They never asked the color of their skin or what tumultuous path they may have been on. They said just one word: yes. Being an interracial family came with its own set of unique challenges, but with grace and pride they'd navigated it beautifully. These children were loved. Not in spite of their dark skin nor because of it. It was simply because they were folded into this family, and, as others had learned before them, once you were in, you were in for life.

"Why are you crying?" Michael, her son-in-law, asked, holding his newborn son in his arms. The baby had just crossed over six weeks old, but Betty had already dubbed him an athlete. He was holding up his head and moving his hands like a baby twice his age. Jules, as a second time mother, had rebounded quickly from labor and birthing. It was nice to have them all back together celebrating Wednesday night dinners as a family again.

When Jules married Michael, Betty knew things would work out. Michael was the perfect match of calm to her daughter's storm. When they had Frankie nine years ago, Betty thought her life was complete. Now she was blessed with four children she considered her grandchildren, and she couldn't imagine life without them.

Surrounded by all this love she figured now was as good a time as any to break her silence about the letter she was holding. "Alma's passed on," Betty managed to say as she patted at the corners of her wet eyes with a handkerchief Bobby had handed her. Clay cut through the group and ran his hand along her cheek. "She told me this letter would be sent after she died. And now here it is. I knew it was coming, but it still doesn't make it any easier."

"I'm sorry, Betty," Clay offered, furrowing his brows. His warm eyes were pools of genuine empathy that Betty dove into. A second husband to a widow was a difficult thing to be. Betty knew that. She gave Clay a lot of credit. Though it was unspoken, there was always a sense of competing with someone's lost love. Her first husband couldn't be replaced in Betty's heart, but, luckily, Clay had never tried that. He found his own way to love Betty and the rest of this unique little group. That was what made him perfect for her.

"Who's Alma, Grammy?" Logan asked as he slipped out of Bobby's arms and brought his small toy soldier over to Betty. He and his twin sister were always lugging around an armful of toys wherever they rambled about. Logan ran his little gun-toting toy across his Grammy's leg. His full lips and plump round cheeks were always tempting Betty to kiss and pinch them. She normally gave in to it no matter how much he squirmed to get away.

"Just like this," Betty said, taking the toy from him and giving it a long look, "Alma was a soldier."

"A Marine like Daddy?" Frankie asked, leaning against Jules and looking up as though she wasn't sure the story could be real.

"No, not in the Marines. Y'all are growing up with your own troubles, but back in my day we had plenty of ours, too. Alma took up a fight that was far overdue, and it nearly cost her everything."

"This is the woman in the letters, right Ma?" Jules asked, looking down at the familiar pink envelope Betty was still clutching. "I've always wondered about those. You've gotten them in the mail for as long as I can remember. She's your pen pal?"

"Yes, but we weren't always just pen pals. Long before that we were living right here in Edenville together. Other than your father, she and her family were the most important people in my life. She reminded me that the things I was busy taking for granted, she was praying for every night. She was my diary. We thought we were just getting by, but I woke up one day and realized we were making memories that would last a lifetime. Most everything y'all know about me came

7

from what I learned from her and her family. I wouldn't be the woman I am today without her."

"Then the world owes her a thank you," Bobby said, offering Betty a warm smile.

Betty pursed her lips and shook her head, looking angry. "The damn world owed her an apology, but she never got it. Our story is one that's blazed into my mind. I can still smell and taste the food we ate. I can still feel the fear and the anger. I can still hear her voice."

"Tell us, Grammy," Frankie pleaded, now looking confused. "Tell us how you knew her." She clasped her hands together, begging with her whole body.

"It's late, dear. Y'all should be heading home. I've got a sink full of dishes to do and a letter to try to read. Maybe some other time." Betty's sadness was starting to cover her like a wooly, suffocating blanket. Rather than hoping everyone would stay and rescue her from it, she wanted to be alone and give in to it. Betty had given out lots of advice in her life. What hardly anyone knew was it had all been given to her first. That's how she knew it was completely acceptable to let the ghosts of the past possess you for a while, as long as you didn't let them stay too long.

"Maybe tomorrow," Piper chimed in, raising her eyebrows as if the statement was a challenge to Betty. That was how Piper was these days now that she had her life together and her feet back under her. She didn't let people get away with being self-destructive by putting off something that was good for them. Even though it was bugging Betty, she was actually proud to see the change in Piper. "The weather is supposed to be beautiful. We can camp out here on the porch, and you can tell us about Alma. It sounds like her story deserves to be told."

"It does," Betty replied in a voice just above a whisper as she put the envelope back to her chest again. It was the closest she could get to holding her friend in her arms, but it was falling miles short. "Tomorrow," she conceded with a nod. "I'll tell y'all about it tomorrow."

"We'll do the dishes tonight, Ma, before we head out. Why don't you just read your letter and rest up." Jules rounded up the kids and started shuffling them back into the house. Everyone but Piper stepped back inside. Her dark chocolate eyes glinted with understanding, and Betty recalled the storm that used to rage in them when they first met.

"I can stay with you while you read it if you like," Piper offered, rubbing Betty's arm affectionately.

"You've really changed over the years. It's amazing to me. You've survived so much and have thrived." Betty tilted her head and smiled.

"Of course I have. I'm one of your strays," Piper teased. That was what they'd taken to calling themselves over the years. It wasn't that far from the truth. In one way or another they were all in need of something when they turned up at Betty's house, and she'd taken them in, either literally or figuratively, depending on their circumstances.

"It's been the greatest pleasure of my life to take in so many. To think I had even the smallest impact on your lives warms me to the core."

"To call the impact you've had small would be the understatement of the decade. If not for your intervention I'm not sure where I'd be. You showed me I was worth the time when I didn't think I was worth anything. You have this way of seeing the best in all of us, and then finding a way to remind us of it when we forget. That's some maternal ninja stuff right there. I don't know if I'll ever be half the mother you have been, but the best choice I ever made was making you Grammy to my twins," Piper said confidently. Piper was never one to lose her composure, unlike Jules, Betty thought, who couldn't tell a knock-knock joke without getting worked up.

Most people would look at Piper and find her to be unemotional and maybe even cold. She never really cried, she never yelled, and she rarely made something out of nothing. But Betty knew inside Piper were all the same feelings and emotions the rest of the world had. She'd just built a stronger cage to keep them in. It's why Betty could appreciate how Piper chose to quietly and privately thank her for the love she'd received.

"I appreciate the kind words and the offer to sit with me. I'm not sure I'll be reading this tonight, dear. You know when you get to the last page of a book that changed your life and you aren't sure how you'll go on once it's over? That's what this feels like. Once I read this, I'll never get another new letter from her. Even if I read it over and over, I'll never be able to read it again for the first time."

"There's no rush," Piper agreed as she squeezed Betty's shoulder and stepped inside the house.

"Maybe tomorrow," Betty sighed as she ran her finger over the words on the front of the envelope. "I miss you already, Alma."

Chapter Two

Staring at the letter for most of the night, Betty let her mind roll through the past. Reflecting on days gone by was usually a happy thing for her, but the part of her life this letter was forcing her to relive wasn't quite as welcoming. It's funny how the mind can be selective in its archiving of memories.

The next day, with a little nudge in the right direction, she stepped into the rundown shed behind her house. It was the keeper of all things she'd tried to forget, so she normally avoided it at all costs. She began digging through boxes of photos and keepsakes. It wasn't long before she was holding the only photograph of her with Alma. For most people who considered themselves lifelong friends, there were albums full of pictures. But this solitary frozen moment in time was the only photographic proof of their friendship.

Brushing off the dust, Betty pushed her glasses up on her nose and inspected it. She hadn't looked at the photo in ages. Shockingly, it was well-preserved, still holding most of its vibrant color. It had nestled for the last couple decades between the pages of an old book. Looking it over she sighed. There she was, standing with one of the best people she had ever known. Her arm was thrown over Alma's shoulders as they laughed at some joke she couldn't recall. There wasn't a single physical thing similar about the two girls. Their features, their hair, the color of their skin: all polar opposites.

The day the photo was snapped focused clearly in Betty's mind as she sifted through the box for more things that might jump-start her memory.

"Everyone's settled on the porch and ready to listen," Clay said in his naturally calming voice as he peeked his head in the shed. That's why Betty fell in love with him—he sprinkled tranquility everywhere he went.

As Betty stepped out of the shed with a box full of yesterdays in her arms, she took stock of the group that had gathered. Bobby was holding the monitor, allowing him to keep an ear out for the twins while they slept upstairs on Betty's bed, and Jules was nursing the baby who was starting to fall asleep.

Everyone was still bustling around as she joined them. Frankie was out in the yard, gathering more twigs for roasting marshmallows, and Betty took the opportunity to address one thing that had been weighing on her. "I'm not sure I want Frankie hearing all this. She still has this picture of the world being all perfect and shiny. I don't want to take that away from her. There are some dark moments she may not be able to understand."

Jules thought for a moment about her daughter's readiness before replying, "If it starts going that direction I'll send her to bed or something. I know dribs and drabs of the stories from your childhood. I know it was no picnic. Frankie can learn from this, we all can. I want her here."

Betty nodded her head in reluctant agreement. One of the hardest things about being Grammy was stepping back and not butting in on every decision. Nine-year-old Frankie was just about two years younger than Betty had been when she met Alma. She'd always believed the best way to keep from reliving the past was to face it, so Frankie could at least face it here with her family.

"I'm as ready as I'll ever be, I suppose." Betty took the hand Clay had extended to her and squeezed it tightly.

All sorts of chairs were squished together so everyone could have a seat. Bobby and Piper settled onto the porch swing. Michael, Jules, and Frankie had three foldout camping chairs pushed together. Clay sat down in his rocking chair and held on to Betty's hand as she sank into her own.

"So we're all covered in bug spray, we've popped popcorn, and we're settled in for the evening. The floor is yours, Betty," Michael said, tossing a blanket over Frankie's legs. His sandy blond hair was now infiltrated by small patches of gray above his temple, but an attractive man like Michael only looked more distinguished as he aged. His wry sense of humor and mischievous smile kept him young.

"This isn't a normal story or anything. It's not something that just has a beginning, middle, and end. It's my life. It's me. How do I express that here?" Betty looked up to the sky as though she might be struck with some inspiration. "I don't know what to say."

Clay chimed in before anyone else could. "I've never known you to be at a loss for words. I half expect the record book people to show up here and take down the date of this unique turn of events." Clay let out a small snicker as he dodged Betty's fake dirty look. They had a playful nature between them, and it kept their relationship exciting.

"Just start from the beginning, Ma," Jules suggested. "It's Friday night. We've got nowhere to be. You start talking, and we'll listen."

"I want you all to promise me you'll be objective. Please be sensitive to the harshness of this story. Don't judge the people who sound horrible. It was a different time." She looked at each of them until they nodded their agreement to her terms. "The beginning, huh? Well I guess that would be around 1961, right here in Edenville. I was eleven years old and spent most of my days going between three places: home, school, and church. My life was as plain as anything. Calling it boring would be an improvement. Same old thing every day, and it made the days feel like they'd last forever.

"Times were different then. News wasn't coming to you minute by minute, flashing on your phone or scrolling on a ticker across your television. Folks got their news from the paper, and it didn't trickle down to us kids much. As far as I knew, the world was a fine place, just like Edenville, but bigger. My folks were quiet. They didn't talk much to me, and they didn't talk much to each other."

"That's sad," Frankie sighed, looking at her parents as though she couldn't imagine them ever ignoring each other.

"The funny thing about life, dear, is you don't know what you don't know. That's all I'd ever been around, so for me it seemed normal. I think that's why I was such a dreamer. I spent most of my free time landing on the moon or going on an African safari in my mind. I could create a world out of the simplest inspiration. But what I didn't realize then was how much I'd missed in the real world. Looking back now, knowing what I know about history and what was really happening all around me, I can't believe I ever thought the world to be a placid place.

"There was so much suffering and oppression, but my biggest problem at the time was trying to manage the blazingly hot summer afternoons without anywhere to swim. My daddy had told me I couldn't go down to the swimming hole anymore, though he didn't offer an explanation. That's another thing that was different back then. The phrase, *because I said so*, was thrown around at least a few times a day. And I never dared question it.

"Wouldn't that be nice?" Michael joked, nudging his daughter. "Frankie debates until she's blue in the face, trying to understand why we decide the things we do."

Betty raised a halting hand at him. "Count yourselves lucky. An inquisitive and confident mind is what makes the world evolve. If people didn't question why things are done, the world would never be forced to improve."

"See?" Frankie said, sticking out her tongue playfully.

"But," Betty cut in with a stern look, "how you use that powerful mind is equally important. The way to be worth listening to is to say the right things, but also leave the wrong things unsaid. That takes restraint and thoughtfulness. It's good to challenge the status quo, but no one will ever take you seriously if you're reckless with your words."

"Yes, Grammy," Frankie said, making a face that illustrated she was up for the challenge. "Is that how you were when you were a kid? Did you talk so people listened like you do today?"

"There were no people to listen, really. I remember feeling very lonely most days. The girls in Sunday school didn't think I was well-behaved enough to spend time with them. The girls smoking cigarettes and cursing behind the schoolhouse didn't think I was bad enough to spend time there. That's how things always were for me. I wasn't enough of any one thing to fit in. I wasn't great at school, but I didn't fail either. I couldn't sing well enough to be in the choir. I couldn't play an instrument with any real talent. I couldn't bake or sew all that well."

"You couldn't bake?" Frankie asked incredulously, completely unconvinced that the woman who cooked for ten people every Wednesday night and ran the kitchen at her very own restaurant couldn't bake. She couldn't imagine a day where Grammy didn't have some kind of kitchen utensil in her hand or a dusting of flour across her clothes.

"I didn't walk out of the womb making a pie crust, no. I was plain and average in all ways. My brown hair wasn't quite curly but not straight either, so I always tied it back in braids. My face wasn't mangled and ugly, but I wasn't winning any modeling contests. So I spent most of my time alone, just dreaming in my own head.

"My mother, Thelma . . . she had always wanted a big family. For most folks that's how it was back then. Being an only child in those days usually meant there was something wrong with either you or your family. It was a sign. But she kept losing babies before they could grow to full term, and it did something awful to her spirit. She never really came back from that. Rather than making her appreciate having me, it seemed to make her resent me. Like I'd done something to her insides while I was in there to make it impossible for her to have more children. That's the way it felt, like she was looking at me, and I could never be enough for her. Every time a woman at our church got pregnant, she sank a little lower.

"My daddy . . . he was something else all together. He was my hero when I was a little girl. I can still remember him hoisting me up on his shoulders at the Fourth of July parade. He worked damn hard as a maintenance man, fixing anything and everything in town that needed fixing. It was well-known if no one else could get your refrigerator repaired, Earl Ray Reynolds could bring it back to life."

"Your maiden name was Reynolds?" Piper asked as she curled her legs up on the porch swing and leaned against Bobby.

"Yes, and when this story is through you'll see why I was happy to rid myself of it as soon as I married Jules's father. It's funny how time can change the meaning of something. How it can twist a reputation from admired to disgraced."

"Grandad was a disgrace?" Jules asked, showing everyone on the porch just how little Betty had shared with her own daughter.

"Not nearly as soon as he should have been. For a long time both my parents were well-liked and respected. My mother was an active member of our church, teaching Sunday school and organizing fundraisers for folks who needed them. She was the first to come by with a pot of soup when someone was sick and the last to leave the school during a bake sale. My daddy was quite active too. He was part of a social group of men revered in our town. His status within the group was one of high stature, and he had worked very hard to earn his position there."

"Did they play cards or something?" Frankie wanted to know, not appearing completely engaged in the story as she twisted a red ringlet of her mother's hair around her finger. It was something she'd done since she was an infant, and every time Betty saw it she smiled.

"They did not play cards, dear," Betty explained, drawing in a deep breath. "They wore white hoods and pretended it wasn't because they knew what they were doing was wrong. They terrorized people while hiding behind religion and righteousness. My daddy, your great-granddaddy, was a loyal member of the Ku Klux Klan."

"Wait, I thought North Carolina was one of the more progressive states in the South, even back then." Bobby sat up a little straighter in his chair. He'd had his own experiences with injustice, and this seemed to unsettle him.

"It was considered such, but that wasn't true. In the early 1960s we had more KKK members than all other Southern states . . ." Betty hesitated for effect, "combined. You heard that right. There were more Klan members right here than all the other states *combined.* It was known around these parts as the heart of Klan country. Which, before I realized what they were doing, was actually something I took great pride in.

"But that pride evaporated and was replaced by an undying desire to understand what was happening around me. Like waking up from a happy dream and realizing it was never real, I awoke from my naïve state and found myself faced with the harsh reality of real life in the South."

"What do you know about the KKK, Frankie? Have you learned about it in school?" Michael asked, leaning down to read his daughter's worried face.

"I don't know much about them. Just, like, they wore hoods and stuff. I've seen a picture. They were bad guys. I didn't know your dad was one," Frankie said, looking half confused and half disgusted, which tugged at Betty's exhausted heart.

"Well, honey, if you stay here, you're about to learn all about my daddy. If you don't think it's something you want to hear, no one would blame you for going in and watching television." Betty pointed to the door. "That goes for any of you, really. I won't paint this story with bright colors or make it into something better than it was."

"I want to know, Grammy. I want to hear about what your life was like. Even if it's bad," Frankie insisted, pursing her lips and steadying her face, trying to look grown-up.

"It is bad, sweetie. But it's also true." She handed over a picture of her clipped from the newspaper. She'd won the local spelling bee and stood proudly next to her trophy. "That's me when I was a little girl. Back when everything was right in the world, or at least I thought so."

"This caption says Beatrice; isn't your name Betty?" Frankie asked, scrutinizing the picture as she scrunched up her nose.

Betty wrung her hands together for a minute as she thought it over. "Beatrice is my birth name, but I haven't been called that since my parents died. It's the name they gave me, but it's not who I am. Sometimes you have to take control of your own life and reinvent yourself in order to be happy. Stick around, and you'll hear all about it."

"Should I open the wine?" Piper asked, gesturing to the bottle on the small table next to her.

Betty sat back in her chair and began rocking slowly. "No honey, someone go get the bourbon."

Chapter Three

1961 – Edenville, North Carolina

"Beatrice, I don't wanna tell you again. Get your skinny butt down here. I need those eggs from Mrs. Winters if I'm going to have your father's birthday cake made tonight."

Reluctantly Beatrice rolled off her bed and shuffled her feet down the long hallway toward her mother's kitchen. The shrill voice calling out to her was nothing new. Her mother always seemed to have a prickly edge when it came to addressing her. She'd never heard either of her parents say they loved her but, worse than that, she never felt like they did. They tolerated each other, and for a long time Beatrice assumed that was how all families were. It wasn't until she started school and saw others that she realized what she was missing.

In general she wasn't finding being eleven all that easy either. It meant she was old enough now to run errands on her own but still too young to do anything fun.

"How many eggs, Mama?" she asked as she rested her elbows on the counter, looking completely bored with the idea of her chore.

"How many ya think? A dozen, of course. There's fifty cents on the counter. It should only cost forty-five cents so bring that nickel back to me. Don't go spending it on penny candy again. Your daddy works too hard for that money for you to be wasting it. Don't be dragging your feet either. I've got the flour all sifted and everything ready to go. I'm just waiting on you." Her mother pointed her finger threateningly.

"Yes, Mama," Beatrice muttered back obediently. But she did drag her feet. She couldn't help it. The two-mile walk to town was boring, and the only thing that made it better was disappearing into her mind and pretending her life was some kind of exciting adventure. She wasn't walking to town to get eggs; this was an expedition across the desert to search for a new species of lizard. Her boring worn-out purple jumper that had grown too tight would transform into the gear of an explorer. Her black and white saddle shoes would become tall boots fit for the wilderness. Sadly, the best thing Beatrice could ever be was usually anything other than what she was.

"It's been four days straight with no sign of the purple-beaked dragon lizard, but I'm not giving up hope." Beatrice put her hand to her brows to block the sun as she scoured the woods to her left and right for a sign of the imaginary creature. When you spent as much time alone as she did you didn't worry much about looking ridiculous. She didn't have much of an audience to embarrass herself in front of. And those people she did see regularly never really seemed to see her. That was why she didn't care if her clothes were snug or worn out. Her mother always bought or sewed her something new when Beatrice got around to asking for it, but it never seemed like a big deal. She saw girls at school who were keeping up with the latest fashions, but she was never one of them. It all seemed like a lot of work, especially if no one would even notice. Plus, like now in the woods, she could imagine herself wearing anything she liked.

"Crazy goofball," a voice rang out as someone raced past her on two wheels. Simpson had been a burr under Beatrice's saddle for as long as she could remember. Two years older than her, he took every chance to give her trouble. He blew spitballs at her in the hallway at school. He made faces at her in church when no one was looking. One time last year he'd slipped a frog into her lunchbox. The joke was on him though, because Beatrice loved frogs. She loved the look of disappointment on his face when she lifted the frog gingerly off her peanut butter sandwich, tucked it in the pocket of her jumper, and named him Simpson, sighting the uncanny resemblance.

But today she wasn't in the mood for him. She was bored and lonely, and the last thing she needed was some teasing. "Shut up, Simpson. Go on," she yelled, kicking a rock at him. In her opinion he was a gangly goofy-looking boy with mud brown hair and hand-me-down clothes. But if you listened to the other cackling girls at school you'd think he was a rock star. They all giggled about his dimples and the sly half smile he flashed. They made up stories, fueling his bad boy imagine that Beatrice could see right through. He wasn't cool and troubled; he was a troublemaker. "Go back to that little old shoe you and your seven brothers live in."

Dragging his toes in the dirt, his bike skidded to a stop a few feet in front of her. "At least I'm not the loony bird out talking to herself. Nobody even likes you."

"Then why are you standing here? Just get going. I've got to get eggs and get back to my mama. Get out of my way." Propping her hands on her hips, she gave him her best dirty look. Something she hadn't perfected yet.

Jumping from his bike and letting it topple over, he stomped toward Beatrice and grabbed a handful of her braid, yanking it hard. He dodged her hand before she could give him a slap. Even as she lunged toward him, Simpson managed to evade her and hop back on his bike.

22

"Loony bird," he called out over his shoulder as he pedaled hard to speed away.

Kicking at some loose rocks on the dirt path, Beatrice clenched her teeth together and grumbled under her breath. She quickly whispered a prayer for forgiveness. She didn't know if there was a patron saint of apologies, but she knew the words she just said, even if they were true, weren't nice to say. She settled on making the sign of the cross as she hurried her pace, remembering the warning her mother had given about not dawdling.

She reached the fence at the edge of the Miller's farm, which meant if she ran she could be in town in a matter of minutes.

Edenville was divided into sections. On the edge of town were houses like Beatrice's, plopped between the farms. Her bloodline hadn't had the money to own much land over the years, so a house on an acre of unfarmable land was the best her grandfather had been able to manage. When he died her father had taken over the deed and done his best to keep the house standing, but it was an uphill battle most days.

Then there were farms set on large plots of rolling hills with mostly rundown fences framing them in. The smell of manure, made worse by the high temperatures in the summer, bowled you over. The barns were all capped with corrugated metal roofs, covered hit-and-miss with paint sandblasted away by soaking rains and blazing heat. Beatrice had always imagined farm life as exciting, but the more farmers she spent time with over the years, the more she realized it was backbreaking work and not quite so glamorous.

Past the farms was Main Street, a bustling culmination of everything anyone could ever need. The street was narrow, barely wide enough for two cars to pass, but on either side of the road were gloriously decorated storefronts, calling patrons in. Bright blue mailboxes lined the corners and brighter signs pointed the way to whatever you needed. Men carrying briefcases made their way to the diner at lunchtime. Women held their babies on their hips and met with the seamstress or the butcher. Old men sat around the tables outside the meatmarket and played checkers. Beatrice loved to see the stakes grow so high that one man would shout and flip the board right off the table. They played with passion.

She didn't know much about the other side of town. She lived on the east side and had never really ventured to the west side. Her father had warned her it wasn't safe, and that was all it took to make her steer clear. She'd heard stories of the haunted shacks and the murderers who lived in those parts. It made her thank her lucky stars to be on this side of town.

Giving a quick pat on the noses of two horses that grazed by the edge of the fence, Beatrice scurried along on her way to Main Street. She was sure the Millers had named the horses, but she'd taken it upon herself to rename them April and Ted.

Taking in a few deep breaths, she imagined herself as an Olympic runner. Pretending to grab the baton from her teammate, she charged forward. With her braided pigtails bouncing wildly and her heart thumping, she made her way down the long hill that led to the edge of Edenville's Main Street.

Edenville was a quiet town where not much of anything seemed to happen. Most people walked to where they had to go; cars were a luxury most of folks couldn't afford. That kept the streets quiet. Beatrice had her favorite places on Main Street, even though she rarely went there without getting in trouble.

The bakery was one of those places. Baker Sam always saved the broken or old cookies and sneaked them into a small brown bag for her. They weren't perfect, but they were something sweet and homemade, which she hardly ever got at home. She decided if she were quick enough getting the eggs, she could sneak in for the cookies and eat them on the way home. As she dreamed of the crumbly, slightly stale, but still good gingersnaps her mouth started to water.

The sidewalks were quieter today than normal, and people seemed to be scattering and heading away from the decorative fountain in the center of the grassy divide. Beatrice felt a nervous cramp in her side. Something seemed very wrong. Slowing her pace to a walk, she curiously inched closer to the place people seemed to be quickly leaving. A bit of excitement would be welcomed, but in an instant she was proved wrong. There were certain types of excitement better left unexplored.

A man was slumped over the side of the fountain. He was a colored man, which was unusual to see on Main Street in the middle of the week. It was an unspoken rule the colored folks only came into town on Mondays and Thursdays. Beatrice didn't know when they had decided that, but she just knew that's how it had been for as long as she could remember. Her daddy had always avoided town on those days, saying it was too full of disease to be walking around. Since Edenville had pretty clear lines dividing where coloreds went and where whites went, Beatrice had spent most of her life around people who looked just like her.

She crept toward the man and could see he was bleeding badly from a cut on his head, which was also quite unusual. The biggest shock of all was the realization that his blood was the same color as her own. She'd always assumed they'd have darker stuff inside them since their skin was so dark.

Her mother had told her time and again to steer clear of the colored folk. They stayed over there, and her people stayed over here. Every now and then, though, one or two would come into the east side of town while Beatrice was there, and she couldn't help but stare hard at them. They looked so different than she and her kin did. She watched them closely and decided they acted pretty much the same as anyone else she knew.

Taking a few steps closer to the injured man, she figured he must have slipped and fallen, knocking his head on the fountain. Looking over her shoulder, she searched for a familiar face to help him, but everyone had moved on. The door to the diner that was always propped open this time of day was shut. The shades in the office building across the way had all been drawn. She thought for a moment that maybe none of this was real. Beatrice spent many afternoons dreaming up all sorts of wild stories to fall into. Could this just be another fantasy?

She pinched the fat of her arm to make sure she was awake. Then it hit her. This must be a message from God. Her mother had often told her to listen closely and she'd hear what God wanted from her. This all made perfect sense. Just this last Sunday Beatrice had learned the story of the Good Samaritan.

This was exactly the same. The Samaritans and the Jews did not spend any time together, and didn't seem to be friends, Beatrice remembered. But when the Samaritan saw a Jewish man who'd been hurt he ignored the fact that the man was different and stopped to help him.

Her mother was always telling her to walk in the light of God and find more ways to be one of his children. Always wanting to please her mother, yet never succeeding, Beatrice took this as a sign to be compassionate and help the man. Jingling the change in her pocket meant for the eggs, she ran into the general store and bought an ice-cold bottle of soda pop and asked Eli, who ran the store, if she could borrow the rag he had over his shoulder. With her supplies in hand she rushed over to the man, who was still propped up and groaning against the fountain. Upon further inspection she realized he couldn't have just fallen here. His injuries were too severe.

"Sir," she whispered, "are you okay?" Her heart was thumping in her chest, but she pushed past her fear and reminded herself how pleased her mother would be when the news got back to her.

His eyes turned toward Beatrice, and she could see they were nearly swollen shut. With all the energy he had left, he waved her off and grunted something that sounded like, "Go on."

"I brought you a soda. It's ice cold. And here's a towel. I can wipe some of the blood away for you," Beatrice offered, trying to sound comforting and unafraid.

He shook his head, but Beatrice heard the words of Jesus at the end of the Good Samaritan story flowing through her: *"Go and do likewise."*

She knelt beside the man and began using the towel to put pressure on the cut on his head. The blood was coming fast but the towel seemed to help. She imagined herself as the Samaritan, stopping to help. Concern for another human, even a stranger or an enemy, was the message that had touched her heart. She had sat there in church and realized that people never noticed her. Perhaps if she were known for something like this act of genuine compassion, people would start to pay attention. "Drink this," she insisted, shoving the glass soda bottle she'd opened into his hand. "If you can walk I'll help you get to Dr. Sherry's office. He'll mend you up."

"No, he won't," the man muttered. "Are you blind or something?"

"I ain't blind. You might be if you don't get your eyes fixed up," she shot back. "They look like they're about to swell shut. You need some tending to."

"Can't you see the color of my skin? Your doctor won't do a thing for me. I need to get back to my people." The more he spoke the more blood seemed to pour from the cut on his head.

"I don't see why you colored folk don't want to be around us white folk. You won't go in our restaurants, and you won't see our doctors," Beatrice huffed, exasperated by his stubbornness. She thought being selfless would be easier, but this man was making it impossible. Didn't he know this was a nice thing she was doing?

Though it seemed completely out of place, the man laughed. Or at least he tried to. It was a low chuckle punctuated by pain, which stopped his laughter abruptly. "Child, oh what it must be like to be so innocent. You need to go on and get out of here." Blood bubbled out of his mouth as he spoke, and Beatrice felt the urgency of the situation growing. If people knew she was this close, this involved, and then the man died right here, she'd be in big trouble.

"I can't just leave you here. I don't know if colored folks know about the Bible or anything, but it tells us to help people. I could tell you the story of the Good Samaritan, and then you'd understand better."

"We know the Bible," he barked back, and Beatrice swallowed hard, scared by the roughness of his voice.

"So then you know I should help you. You know what compassion is, right? My daddy says you people don't have the same kinds of brains as we do, so it's okay if you don't know the Word." Beatrice tried to keep her voice slow and gentle so he could understand the best he could.

"Child, go. It ain't your fault you don't know any better, but people are coming over here. You need to go on."

"I'm gonna hold this towel on your head until someone fetches the doctor. I don't care if you don't wanna see a white doctor." Whatever the man's holdup was about white people, he'd have to put it aside she decided.

"Beatrice," a familiar and angry voice rang out from behind her. "What the hell are you doing?" Though she couldn't see his face behind his white hood, she knew it was her daddy.

"Daddy, this man fell down. We need to fetch the doctor." She'd forgotten something important her daddy had always told her about when he was in his Klan robe. Even if she knew it was him, she wasn't supposed to tell anyone. The group was very important and for some

29

reason they couldn't have anyone knowing who they were. She remembered instantly, as he cut the space between them with ferocity, she'd broken that rule and was in trouble.

Eli stepped outside just as her father reached her. "Is that my damn towel covered in this animal's blood? You got his filthy blood everywhere," Eli raged.

Her father grabbed her neck and yanked her away from the injured man. "You fool," he fumed. "You don't touch him. You don't help him. He is an animal. A criminal. That's why we beat him. He's like a dog that bit someone."

"He bit someone?" Beatrice asked, looking the man over as her father dragged her farther and farther away.

"No, dummy," her father hissed. "He drank out of the whites only fountain as if he's the same as us. He knew better. It's bad enough we have to let them walk down Main Street and breathe the same air as us. I'll be damned if they're going to dirty up our things."

"You beat him for getting a drink?" Beatrice cried, hunching under the pain of her father's tight grip on her neck.

"You're not a baby anymore, girl. Your mama can say all she wants that you're too slow in the head to be told about the world, but obviously if I don't you'll run our family's name through the mud. I don't ever want to see you helping, talking to, or being anywhere near one of them ever again. I have worked my whole damn life to keep them in their place so the world can be worth living in for you. Don't go undermining all my work and the work of the Klan by treating them like people."

"Aren't they people?" Beatrice asked as they made their way past the fence at the Miller's farm. She wanted to see if the horses were still standing by the fence for a pat on the nose again. Before she could be grateful for the release of her neck, she was whacked hard across the face by her father's hand.

"How can you be this old and not know this? They ain't people. If I ever hear you talking like this again, you'll get the beating of your life," he snarled. The anger raging in his grey-blue eyes was unnerving.

Nothing about this afternoon made sense to Beatrice. All she knew was she didn't want to be beaten, but something was about to make that inevitable. "I forgot Mama's eggs," she cried in a sudden panic.

"Then you better go out to the field and bring in a switch. When she hears what you did, and you come back empty-handed, you'll be in for it," her father grumbled.

"But I was trying to be like the Good Samaritan. I don't understand." The fear of the inevitable whooping filled Beatrice's eyes with tears.

"You better start understanding right quick. If they know their place and follow the rules, we put up with them. But one toe out of line and we give them what they deserve. And nowadays it's not just about them but anyone who tries to help them, too, the way you just did. Like a fool. That's what this is all about," he said, gesturing to his white robe. "I do this for you."

For the rest of the walk home they were both silent. Beatrice hung her head and cried, knowing she was about to face the wrath of her mother when all she'd wanted to do was show her how she could walk with God. Being eleven was proving impossible. Nothing made sense anymore, and all she ever got lately was a good walloping.

Danielle Stewart

"I'm sorry, Daddy, I didn't know," she apologized, feeling like she must be the stupidest child in the world.

"You got his blood on your clothes. We'll have to burn them tonight," he retorted coldly.

"Yes, Daddy," she agreed as she looked down at the bright red blood that rimmed the edge of her jumper. She didn't understand any of this, but she could tell she better figure it out soon.

Chapter Four

Beatrice had thought there would be nothing worse than the whooping she received that night, but she was wrong. The way she was treated at school the weeks after was far harder to deal with then the wallops on her rear end from her mother. After word of what she'd done had traveled around town, Beatrice had been called names, had gum stuck in her hair, and had been ignored by anyone who wasn't harassing her. The teachers wouldn't call on her even when her hand was the first one to go up to answer a question. The only two things she experienced now were teasing and feeling invisible; she couldn't sort out which one hurt more.

With her head down and her heart aching, she muddled through the school days then dragged herself through her front door every evening, knowing it wouldn't be much better. Her parents weren't calling her names and they weren't completely ignoring her, but disappointment was constantly painted on their faces.

Her stomach ached most of the time and food tasted like sawdust in her mouth. She'd always been lanky, but now she was getting bony. Most days she did everything she could to find a place to be alone after school. Today she decided to take the long way home. The very long way.

Cutting through the woods behind the Dorit's farm, she weaved her way to the brook and followed it north toward her house. She turned left after she saw the old cemetery she used to avoid at all costs. Suddenly the dead didn't seem quite as scary as the living. A bunch of old headstones couldn't call her names or spit in her food.

After walking for what felt like an hour, she heard the unmistakable sound of a twig cracking beneath someone's foot. She dropped low, squatting and slowing her breathing as she tried to find the source of the noise. Had one of those jerks from school spotted her heading into the woods and followed her so they could tease her again for her mistake? Would they pour soda on her and tell her to give it to her colored friends? Didn't they know she didn't have colored friends? She'd barely known a single one of them her whole life, but now the way people were acting you'd think she was out jumping rope and having cookies with them every day.

When she heard nothing for a minute she thought of standing, but something told her to stay put. Something in her gut just kept saying, *Not yet. Don't move yet. It's not time.* Then she heard it: a scream followed by a body bolting by her. It was a black girl moving so quickly she wasn't paying attention to branches that were slapping her across the face. The girl's foot caught on a log and she dropped to the ground with a thud that told Beatrice she'd likely had the wind knocked out of her. Chasing behind her was a familiar face. Simpson had his baseball bat slung over his shoulder as he closed the gap between him and the fallen girl. Beatrice could recognize him from a mile away. He had abnormally large brown eyes and his hair did this spikey, untamed thing, making him look far more interesting than he was.

"Stop," Beatrice shouted, tossing herself between them before Simpson could reach the girl. His body slammed into hers, and they both toppled to the ground.

"What the hell are you doing out here, Beatrice?" Simpson barked, jumping to his feet and brushing the dirt off his tattered hand-me-down pants.

"I'm walking home," she explained, turning toward the little girl and extending her hand to help her up. "Are you hurt?" she asked, looking the girl over once she was on her feet. She had her black hair parted in three different spots and pulled back into tight braids punctuated at the bottom with pink plastic clips. When she spoke Beatrice saw her smile had multiple holes where her baby teeth had fallen out. Her dress, which was now soiled, had matched the clips perfectly. It was trimmed with lace at the sleeves and hem, and Beatrice could tell it had been made with great care. Her round plump lips, framed perfectly by even plumper cheeks, were quivering with fear. Beatrice had never seen such pretty eyes before. They were rich and shiny like molasses and shimmered beneath the tears gathering in them. They seemed bottomless, and it made Beatrice want to lean in and examine them further. As the girl blinked nervously, Beatrice watched her long curled-up lashes catch some of the drops and hold them. The girl finally offered only a small, nearly imperceptible nod to Beatrice to let her know she was fine.

"Beatrice, what the hell? Are you really that thick? You didn't learn anything from last month did you?" Simpson shoved Beatrice aside with a force unlike any of the playful teasing the two of them had done in the past. He was angry. "She needs to go on. Now."

Shoving him back, Beatrice let all the fury that had been building in her over the last month show on her face. "She's a little girl. You're going to beat her with a bat?"

"I got lost," the girl whimpered, dropping her head obediently like a dog to its master. "I'm sorry. I didn't mean to." Her voice was quivering, and that only made Beatrice's rage grow.

"God tells us to love everyone," Beatrice countered with her chin held high. "She's a lost little girl. She deserves mercy."

"Shut up, Beatrice," Simpson growled, looking over his shoulder and biting at his lip nervously.

"You can't seriously think you should beat her with that bat because she got lost near your farm?" she shot back, eyeing Simpson's hesitation. Surely if he was going to do it he'd have done it by now.

"You're a retard, Beatrice. You must be. I know your mama and daddy can barely read and you don't have no television, but how can you not know what's going on in the world? It ain't just about them anymore." He gestured over to the little girl with the tip of the bat and sent her jumping nearly out of her skin. "They're stringing up whites now, too. Shooting them. Burning them. White people out there marching with them, trying to get them the vote; they're getting killed, too. You can't help them. You ain't supposed to." Simpson dropped his bat to his side, but his face was twisted up and angry like he was trying to explain to a horse how to eat with a fork.

"I don't get it. Why does everyone hate them so much?" Beatrice demanded, balling her fists together and stomping her foot in frustration. "I'm tired of being dumb about all this stuff. I want to know."

"It's complicated," Simpson replied as he brushed his hand over his dark brown hair. She saw gold flecks in his eyes that had previously been masked by a fierce anger, and they now caught the light that filtered down through the trees.

"I don't know what I'm supposed to do," Beatrice said with a shake in her own voice now. She was exhausted. Sick of feeling tired and stupid.

"You don't have to do a damn thing and you're mighty lucky for that," Simpson explained with an edge back in his voice. "No one is looking to you to do anything. No one is handing you a white hood. You're a girl, all you gotta do is keep your mouth shut and stay out of the way. Count yourself lucky for that and go on home."

"I ain't gonna let you hurt her. You'll have to hurt me too. There ain't no way I'm going home knowing you're gonna beat on her." Beatrice stuck out her chin defiantly. Surely this was different than the man on Main Street she'd tried to help. Her father couldn't possible agree that this little girl, who'd accidently gotten lost, should be beaten by a boy so much larger than she was. The situations were completely different, and she tried to convince herself that she was doing the right thing.

Simpson drew in a deep breath as though he was trying to calm his temper. "You don't know what you're doing, Beatrice. This ain't kid shit anymore. We ain't horsing around in the schoolyard. The world isn't what you think it is. You have a choice to make. We all do. People don't want any kind of mixing with colored folks. They're willing to do anything to keep that from happening. And you're either with them or you're dead. That's your choice."

"I ain't leaving her. You wanna hit me with that thing, then go ahead." Beatrice closed her eyes, blocked the girl with her body, and braced for impact.

Gritting his teeth and growling, he leaned in close to Beatrice's face. "You know damn well I ain't gonna do that. But it ain't me you gotta worry about. There's four other boys and two of my brothers just a half mile behind me, and they won't think twice about it."

Looking past his shoulder, genuine fear began to set in. She'd known Simpson all her life. He'd be unlikely to really raise a hand to her, but these other boys wouldn't.

"Run, Beatrice. This is the one and only time I'll ever cover for you. You pull shit like this again, and I won't stand in anyone's way. Just take her with you and run." Simpson lifted his bat and used it to point in the direction they should head.

Her legs didn't instantly respond as she thought they would. Instead she froze for a moment until he barked at her again, "Run!"

Latching onto the girl's hand, she spun away from Simpson and headed toward the west side of Edenville. She ignored the pain of whipping branches and the pinch of a cramp in her side. Nothing would slow her down, for any pain she was feeling would be dulled in comparison to what would happen if they were caught.

"I know where I am now," the girl mustered through exhausted breaths. "My house is just over that hill." She tugged Beatrice's arm and, knowing there was an end in sight, felt a much-needed burst of energy. As their tired feet pounded the dirt, they came to the edge of the woods and stood atop a hill. Beatrice looked down over the gully and realized where she was. This was the west side of Edenville. This was where she was never supposed to venture. Every story she'd ever heard about the place began circling her mind like vultures. Sprinkled across the grassless field and blocked by overgrown trees were dozens and dozens of shacks. The dirt road that led into the ravine was only wide enough for one car, and deep holes had been cut in it by rain that raced down toward the shacks. There were no real roads that led up to each place, just paths created from multiple passes over the mud.

All the shacks looked like they were fighting gravity and a few had lost, caving in on themselves like a loaf of bread that hadn't had enough time in the oven. Beat up trucks and old furniture littered the open spaces. Fences that were missing full sections did their best to divide each property and give the façade of privacy.

The entire place was sad. That was the best way Beatrice could describe it. It made her feel sad. There were no vibrant colors; everything was the dingy brown-gray of weathered wood or the burnt copper of rust. No flowers bloomed in window boxes; the windows barely looked like they could hold themselves in place. A few skinny dogs roamed and a few skinnier kids chased them.

"Is this where you live?" Beatrice asked, raining pity down like a waterfall on this poor child.

"That one there," the girl answered with a big smile. "We live in one of the nice ones with the good windows and a sturdy porch. We'll have to run fast; we're tucked away real good behind those trees so no one should see you—but just in case."

It was the nicest shack, but that was like being the best pup in a bad litter. Its dirt front yard looked well kept, no garbage was strewn across it. It was tucked away, and more private, but that was the extent of its luxuries.

As they took off in a sprint down the steep hill, Beatrice felt as though she were flying, and not in a good way. Racing toward this unfamiliar and new world felt out of her control.

"Alma Mae, where on God's green earth have you been? You had me as worried as a long-tailed cat in a room full of rocking chairs." The woman's voice came echoing from the porch. It was brash, but when they grew closer Beatrice could see her face was soft as she opened her arms wide. The little girl plowed right into her and buried her face in her chest. Beatrice felt suddenly out of place as they all stood on the front step in silence.

Staring down at her shoes, she kicked at a pebble and contemplated just turning around and going home. But the stitch in her side was still aching.

"I got lost, Mama. There was this boy with a baseball bat, but this girl, she saved me," Alma explained through tears.

"Saved you?" the broad-shouldered woman asked as she looked Beatrice from head to toe appraisingly. Her face was round like her daughter, her arms thick and chocolate colored. Nothing about her was petite, but somehow she was still incredibly feminine. It was in the curve of her hips and the fullness of her mouth. Her hair was pinned back with much care, leaving perfectly sculpted waves framing her face. Even with an apron on, a broom in her hand, and mud-covered boots, she looked elegant.

She was larger than Beatrice's own meek mother in every way. Her voice was louder. Her dress was more colorful, and her presence could be felt even when she was silent.

"She told that boy she wasn't going to let him beat me. Then she grabbed my hand, and we ran the whole way here," Alma explained, her words coming quickly and plowing into each other.

"Girl, did you make sure they weren't following you? Are they coming this way?" the woman asked nervously, clutching her daughter tightly.

The fear that spread across her face made Beatrice's heart skip a beat. It wasn't often that a grown-up in her life showed any kind of true alarm. It was wholly unsettling.

"They didn't, Mama. I watched. No one's coming." Alma spoke into her mother's shoulder, clearly not ready to let go. "We ran so fast, Mama."

"That's good, girl. You gotta be fast. Now come on in the house so I can clean up those little cuts on your face," the woman instructed as she brushed her thumb across her daughter's cheek.

"What about her?" Alma asked, pointing over at Beatrice who was still feeling as though she were intruding.

"Go on home," the woman said, almost as a question.

"She needs a drink or something first. She just ran near-on two miles. Plus those boys might still be out there," Alma insisted, looking at her mother as though she were being unreasonable.

"You know full well she can't be coming in our house," the woman replied with a choked out laugh. "I'm grateful for what she did, but it don't work like that."

"Ain't it worse for her to be standing out here where anyone can see her? Seems like inside at least her white skin ain't catching the sun and glowing for everyone to see. We've got the most private house here, but should we count on that?"

Beatrice looked down at her arms and then up at the sun as though she had some kind of magic reflecting power she didn't know about.

"Don't be smart," the woman scolded, swatting gently at her daughter's backside as she reluctantly waved Beatrice to come in the house.

Beatrice hesitated only a second then looked around and hurried herself in the front door of the dirt-floor shack. She'd never been in a house without a real floor before. The place was old, and the kitchen didn't have a single updated appliance in it. The stove was wood-burning and clunky looking. The icebox wasn't even electric, which meant they still had ice delivered to them. She didn't know anyone who was still doing that. The beams of the roof were exposed and barely looked like it could keep rain out if needed. How could anyone live like this, she wondered.

"I'm Winnie. This here is my daughter, Alma. What's your name?" Pouring out a glass of water from a pitcher that sat on the crooked kitchen table, Winnie eyed Beatrice again.

"My name is Beatrice, but I hate that name," she admitted for the first time out loud. No one had listened to her in so long she had forgotten anyone might actually care what she thought. "It's my grandmother's name, and she was a mean old coot. Who wants to be named after somebody mean?"

"Ha," Winnie hollered. "Well ain't that the truth. So why not shorten it a bit. You could be Bea. Or Betty. I had a cousin named Betty, she was sweet as a peach pie."

"I could be named after her." Beatrice smiled, but it slipped off her face when Winnie slammed her hand down on the table with a loud laugh.

"I can see the resemblance," she jested. "Now, Betty, tell me what in the world you were doing standing between my baby girl and a baseball bat? Don't you know any better?"

"I'm starting to think I might be dumb or something. Everyone keeps telling me how the world is and how I'm supposed to act and feel and stuff, but I don't. It keeps confusing me and I keep getting everyone all mad." Betty felt tears dripping down her cheeks. Maybe she was just tired from the running, but really it was her heart that felt tired. She didn't bother crying when the girls at school cut her straps on her jumper. She didn't cry when her mother kept sending her to bed earlier and earlier every night. But here she couldn't help it.

"Girl, why are you crying? Don't be doing all that in here. You'll turn our dirt floor to mud," Winnie joked, but it was clear by the look in her large round eyes she felt bad for Betty.

She blinked away the tears and stared at Winnie, taking in the differences in her features. Winnie's nose was flat and wide, her nostrils flaring when she let out her hardy laugh. Her teeth were pearly white and when she flashed them her whole face lit up. "I'm sorry," Beatrice sniffled, trying to wipe the tears away. But they just kept coming, as did her confessions. "I'm just so lonely. Ever since last month nobody will talk to me. And if they do it's just to call me names and shove me around. My own kin thinks there's something wrong with me, so there must be. I keep getting told one thing and doing another. I never should have given that man that soda, but he was so hurt."

"That was you?" Alma asked, her dark molasses eyes going wide. "You're the little girl who helped Amos after they beat him?"

"No," Winnie said, shaking her head in disbelief. "You must be joking with me here."

"I saw him lying there all beat up, and I just thought about what I learned at church. I thought God would want me to help him. But now everyone is telling me you ain't really people so God doesn't care about you the same way." Betty spoke with flailing arms as she paced around the tiny old kitchen trying to get it all off her chest.

"We is too," Alma bit back angrily. "God loves me just fine."

"Hush your mouth, child. It isn't her fault that's what they teach her. How's she supposed to know if that's all she ever hears?" Winnie reminded her daughter.

Betty was nearly sobbing now, her wet eyes darting around the room as she tried to gather her thoughts. "So if God does care about you then I'm supposed to. The Bible says that clear as day. But I'm supposed to honor my mother and father, too; the Bible says that. My daddy says you're dirty. That you're dumb folks who don't deserve the same things we have. If they let you vote then you'll take over the country and muck it all up. I don't think I want that to happen either. How am I supposed to know what to do?"

"You are a dumb-dumb," Alma said, balling her hands into fists, looking ready for a fight. She'd been the one to insist Betty come in, and now it looked like she was ready to toss her out. This was the problem with the world as far as Betty could see it. No one made any sense to her. They all changed their minds too quickly.

"Alma, shut your lips. Let the girl get it all out," Winnie demanded as she shot her hand up and halted her daughter from saying another word.

"Simpson, the boy with the baseball bat. I've known him since we were in diapers. Now it's like I don't know him at all. My daddy, I thought he was just in this club or something, and now I'm hearing all this stuff about who the Klan is."

"Your daddy is Klan?" Winnie asked, dropping the towel she was holding to the floor. The shock in her eyes was enough to rattle Betty to the core.

"Yes," Betty answered meekly, still unsure of the ebb and flow of this conversation and what it seemed to be doing to them.

"Girl, you need to drink up that water and be on your way. You can't be caught here. Not in my house," Winnie insisted as she moved around the kitchen nervously. "If I'd had known that from the start I wouldn't have let you in."

"What else can they do to me? Everyone already treats me like I'm a leper. I don't care if they know I'm here." Betty shrugged, trying to look confident and brave.

"It ain't what they do to you, dummy," Alma cut in, "it's what they'd do to us if they found a little white girl here who belongs to the Klan. It don't matter what you tell them you were doing here. They'd have us hung up in a tree before we even had time to explain."

"I'm sorry you're having a hard time," Winnie said, seeming to center herself again. "You seem like you have a good heart. But these times aren't for people with good hearts. It's too dangerous for that. You need to go on home and do whatever your daddy tells you to. Don't be letting any of those other thoughts in your head. I thank you for what you did for my daughter today, but next chance you have to do something like that again—don't."

"I don't belong anywhere," Betty croaked as she placed her glass on the table and shuffled toward the door. "If I try to be a Christian my family will hate me, and everyone I know will torture me. When I try to help, even you people don't want me around." Betty used her sleeve to wipe her eyes. "And if I don't help, if I stand by and watch it happen, I'll hate myself. There ain't no way to get it right."

"You're just a little girl. I bet you're what, eleven?" Winnie asked with softness in her eyes again. She was clearly as tormented and confused as Betty was, and that brought Betty an odd comfort. Being alone in anything, even sadness, feels terrible. "Alma is only ten. You both got a long bit of growing up to do. When you're a big girl, a grown person, you can do more if you still want to. But right now, little girls can't get anything done. Not in this kind of world. You just need to keep your head down long enough. Things will either change or you'll get big enough to try to help change them yourself. But it ain't for little girls to be worrying about."

"So you're saying just listen to my daddy? Listen to the folks telling me what I should do?" Betty asked, looking desperate for anyone to give her the answer.

"Yes," Winnie nodded. "That's what you do."

"They'll tell me to kick a man like Amos. They'll tell me to hold Alma down while they teach her a lesson for wandering onto their property. I should turn my nose up to the woman who cleans house for the Davis family and act like she's not there. I should stand with my arms linked together with my family, blocking the way of anyone looking to vote. I don't want to do all those things, Winnie. I don't want to." Betty's tears fell again and her shoulders slumped over. For a brief second there was no color in this room. Just a terrified child and a comforting mother.

Winnie pulled Betty in for a hug so tight she nearly lost her breath. The warmth of her arms around her did the trick. The last time she'd been hugged was the day her mother had her first miscarriage. Betty had been a form of comfort for her mother but soon that twisted to something much different, and hugging was no longer something they did.

Her hug with Winnie was only a few heartbeats long, but for that time Betty felt safe.

"I don't know what I'm supposed to tell you," Winnie admitted. "There's no answers in this world. Even if we wish there were, these problems are as old as time and they aren't going anywhere."

"What do you do when you feel like this," Betty asked, keeping her face pressed against Winnie.

"'Round here we cook. Sometime a recipe is the only thing we can control. Sometimes things feel better on a full belly." Winnie nodded her head and smiled down at Betty, trying to brighten the darkness of reality.

"Really?" Betty asked, astonished at how easy that answer was. Could everything really be solved just like that?

"No, not really. All of your problems are still waiting for you on the other side; you're just more ready to deal with them if you've been fed properly. You know anything about cooking?" Winnie asked, raising an eyebrow at Betty.

"No, but I'm plenty skilled in eating," Betty said with a grin, the first big smile she'd had all day.

"Girl, in this house if you ain't mixin' it and you ain't fixin' it, you ain't eatin' it. Go on and wash your hands in that basin, and I'll show you how to make the pecan pie we're having for dinner tonight."

"Yes ma'am," Betty called out, regaining her voice as the tears stopped falling.

"Now hurry up though. You need to be well out of here before my husband comes home. He'll drop dead of a heart attack if he see's a little white girl wearing one of my aprons."

Betty's eyes lit with excitement as she clapped her hands together. "I get an apron?"

"You do, but once you have it on it means you gotta do your share of the work." Winnie pointed her finger at Betty in mocked sternness.

"I promise," Betty assured, her eyes wide with enthusiasm. "Thanks for being my friends."

"We aren't friends," Alma said curtly as she moved to the other side of the kitchen and readied herself to help with the cooking.

"Alma," Winnie spat back, not seeming to need any more words than that to be understood by her daughter.

"But we ain't enemies either," Alma shrugged, tossing an apron over to her. For the first time in a month, Betty's stomach didn't ache.

Chapter Five

"Betty," she said to herself. She loved the way it sounded on her lips. The way the new name made her feel. Reborn. The skip had returned to her step as she cut through the woods and returned to Alma's house the following day. She'd paid close attention on her way home last night to be sure she'd remember the way. All day at school while people acted as though she were invisible, she daydreamed of the pecan pie they'd made the day before. She could almost taste the sweet sugary syrup they'd drizzled over the top of the pie. Just like yesterday, she'd stop feeling left out and start smiling again. All she had to do was make it to Alma's house.

At the top of the ridge she looked down at the tiny house and smiled. She knew she needed to be careful approaching the door as to not draw attention to her. There were no houses close by to Alma's, and if she stood up here for a minute she could make sure no one was lurking around. It was foolproof.

Once she was satisfied the area was clear, she set off in a run toward the front door. She wasn't dumb anymore. Winnie had shed a little light on how things worked in this world, and Betty was determined to be careful. With a quick and quiet knock on the door she held her breath, looking over her shoulder again and again.

When the door did open it was just a crack, with Alma's little eye peering through. "What in the hell?" she stammered, swinging the door open and yanking Betty all the way in.

"What are you cussing about?" Winnie asked, rounding the corner to the kitchen, a batch of laundry under her arm. "What in the hell?" she exclaimed, parroting her daughter's words.

"What?" Betty asked, looking down over her floral patterned dress as if she'd spilled something on it that was drawing this type of reaction.

"Why are you here? You can't just be showing up out of nowhere," Winnie scolded, tossing the laundry on the table as she folded her arms over her chest. It was all very different than the open arms Betty had felt just yesterday.

"But we cooked together. We made the pie. I thought I'd come back today and we could eat some together." Betty couldn't understand why they were acting as though she'd done something wrong. Had yesterday meant nothing to them? Was it just some prank they were playing on her like everyone else in her life?

"We didn't invite you back. I thought you'd have noticed that." Alma moved to stand next to her mother and folded her arms the same way. At the sight of that, Winnie groaned and changed her posture, letting her arms drop down to her side. She nudged her daughter to do the same. She might be angry, but she didn't want to be a bad example for Alma, and Betty could appreciate that.

"You gotta learn how things work, little girl," Winnie continued, though the edges of her face were softer now. "You aren't out here visiting your cousin. You don't just walk up and knock on the door whenever the mood strikes you. I told you, you coming around here is too dangerous for all of us. Yesterday you were having a hard day and I felt for you, but I think you should go on home now. I'm grateful for how you helped my Alma but you can't be here."

"It wasn't just a hard day." Betty forced her voice to stay level even though she wanted to cry again.

Alma's forehead crinkled as she furrowed her brows at Betty. "You been treated bad for like a month. We get treated like that every day."

"That seems like a good reason to be my friend then. If everyone is treating us bad we should be good to each other. I've been trying to read stuff over the last couple weeks since I helped that man by the fountain. I've been trying to understand what's going on better. I'm trying," Betty said earnestly as her eyes pleaded for a lifeline.

Alma rocked her head back and forth with attitude as she explained the world to Betty. "In a couple weeks everyone's gonna stop calling you names. They'll look at you and forget. Ain't nobody gonna look at me and forget my skin is black. And right about that time when they start being nice to you again, I'd bet my mother's biscuit recipe you'll forget all about us."

With a light thwack to the back of the head, Winnie silenced her daughter. "Don't go betting my biscuit recipe on anything. That's sacred. And quit being so mean to this little girl. She saved your behind yesterday, and I don't know if you even said a proper thank you. Well, go on."

"Thank you," Alma said through pursed lips as she rubbed the back of her head where her mother whacked her.

"So I can stay?" Betty asked clapping her hands together in excitement.

"Why do you want to?" Winnie asked, still not looking convinced. "Why do you want to be here with us?"

"I've been giving it a lot of thought. I was up most of the night. I don't want to be ignorant. Yesterday you said some things I never heard before. There are things I thought about all colored folks, and you showed me they were lies. I want to know the truth. All of it. I want you to tell me everything." Betty's eyes were wide, and her face was lit with hunger to learn.

"Hell no," Winnie said waving her hands like she was shooing the idea away. "What do you want me to be? Your conscience? Your history teacher? Your priest? I'm not going to sit around and tell you everything you know is a lie. I don't want that burden."

"I want to know what's true. You could tell me," Betty pleaded.

"Did you know I'm a teacher? Have been for over a decade. Everything I believe in is based on shaping young minds. But this, no, this is too much. You know how dangerous it would be?" Winnie shook her head adamantly as though she were trying to keep the idea from getting hold of her brain.

"Isn't it more dangerous to have bigots and ignorant people running around? You could do something about that. You could tell me how it really is," Betty countered with a victorious grin. She'd spent most of the night thinking through her response to the argument she might receive when she asked Winnie to teach her. She was proud of what she'd come up with.

Winnie drew in a deep breath and looked down at Betty as though she was wearing on her last nerve. "There'd be rules," she huffed out, sinking into a kitchen chair. "We'd need to come to an understanding about things first."

"Yes, ma'am," Betty answered, her eyebrows rising in hopeful anticipation.

Winnie lost her breath for a moment, and Alma choked a bit, both of them looking at Betty again in that way that made her feel like she had spinach in her teeth or something.

"What? Did I do something wrong already?" Betty asked sheepishly.

"No," Winnie said, leaning over and closing her daughter's mouth that had dropped wide open. "You're just the first white girl to ever call me ma'am. I've been called lots of names in my day, but that isn't one of them."

"Want me to stop?" Betty asked, wondering what else she was supposed to call her.

"It's mighty nice of you to do it, but you can just call me Winnie. I think that'll do fine. Now we need to go over the rules."

"Yes, ma'am. I mean yes, Winnie."

"You will not come down here unannounced like you're delivering us a newspaper. When you leave, we'll talk about the next time you come. You'll come in through the woods and go 'round to the door on the side of the house. It's your job to make sure nobody follows you or sees you coming or going. And most important, you don't tell anyone you're here. Not your priest. Not your best friend. Not your mama. Even if you believe someone won't think nothing of it. They will. There's no wiggle room on that one. If you care about keeping us from getting hurt, you'll take that seriously."

"Cross my heart," Betty promised.

"There's more. And this one is a big one. I'll answer your questions the best I know how. And I'll be as honest with you as I can be. But what I won't do is fill your head with things so you can turn around and think you're a Freedom Rider or something. You are a child. You aren't gonna go out and fix everything. You aren't gonna take up the fight. I'll tell you what's happening in the world but I'm not telling you to go take up the cause. Can you keep that straight between those two pigtails of yours?"

"Yes, I just have one question," Betty chirped as she slid into the seat across from Winnie. "What's a Freedom Rider?"

"I'll answer your question when you answer one for me," Winnie said, narrowing her eyes and scrutinizing Betty. "You are eleven years old. Your daddy is in the Klan. How in the world do you know so little about the way things work?"

Betty felt her cheeks tingle with embarrassment. She wasn't blind to the fact that she was different than the other kids. She wasn't deaf to the chatter about her being a very young eleven. But explaining that out loud felt like she had a mouth full of cotton.

"I'm in my head a lot. Mama calls me a daydreamer and Daddy calls me dummy. There isn't anything wrong with me really; well, I don't think so. I score average on all my school stuff. It's just that, every chance I get, my brain just goes into another world all its own. I guess I haven't been paying attention. Plus my folks don't talk much to me. Mama tells me about religion, and Daddy is just quiet."

With a knowing nod Winnie folded her hands and rested them on the table. "I'll tell you what I know about the Freedom Riders while we pit some cherries."

"Cherry pie is my favorite," Betty squealed making a funny face at Alma.

"Don't get too excited," Alma shrugged. "Mama has a rule for everything, including pies. No eating pie until you know how to make the whole thing yourself."

"Then I'll be a fast learner."

Chapter Six

Betty had a notebook tucked under her arm as she charged out of the woods, down the hill, and into Alma's side door. She was out of breath as she stumbled through, but, like always, her adrenaline kept her from slowing down.

"I'll never get used to you just barging through that door," Alma groaned as she carried an armful of laundry to the table to start folding it. Betty knew she was expected to help so she grabbed a towel and got to work.

"I brought a notebook today so I can write stuff down. That helps me remember," Betty said with a prideful smile.

"Mama will make a rule about that. She won't want you walking around with book full of the stuff she's told you. It won't matter today though. I don't know where she is."

"What do you mean you don't know where she is?" Betty asked, feeling frustrated she might not get what she came for.

"She was at school today, teaching like she always does. I saw her in the hallway twice on my way to recess. But then when I walked home from school, she wasn't here. She must've had to stay after school for something," Alma said with a casual shrug.

"Aren't you worried? Something might've happened to her. We should go out looking." Betty dropped the towel she was folding to the table and moved toward the little window at the front of the shack. She pushed aside the thick Army blanket they'd hung up as curtains and peered outside.

"You really are dense. My mama would whoop me seven ways to Sunday if I went out looking for her. She'd tell me she's a big girl and can handle herself. She wants me right here after school. Just look at what happened last time I disobeyed. I nearly got my block knocked off by some hillbilly with a baseball bat, and I got stuck with you."

"What happened? Why are you being so mean to me now? You're the one who invited me in here that first day. You insisted your mama let me in." Betty felt her cheeks pink as she was reminded Alma wasn't quite as welcoming as Winnie had become. "Why don't you like me? I'm nice to you. I don't treat you like other white folks treat you. I help you with your chores while I'm here. I saved you, you should like me." Betty had grown accustomed to not being liked. Her whole life she'd felt different from everyone around her. The best shot she had was wearing people down. Being around until they warmed up to her. But so far with Alma it hadn't worked.

"It was easier before when I was just supposed to not trust any white person *ever*. That was the rule my mama gave me. Keep to myself. Be respectful. Apologize for being in the way. Now you've got me wondering which ones are the bad apples and which ones might be all right. I liked it better when I didn't have to think about it." Alma folded the clothes on the table quickly, looking like she'd rather be anywhere else. But Betty knew the tiny shack left nowhere to hide.

"Sorry for making you use your brain," Betty shot back jokingly. "You should know, though, I'm not going anywhere. My plan is to keep coming here and keep trying to understand the world best I can. You don't have to like me. You'd have lots of company standing in that line with you, 'cause most people don't like me." Betty kept her chin raised high as she folded the last towel. "I can even help you with your school work if you'd like."

"I don't need any help. I'm real good at fractions and history. I get perfect grades," Alma shot back, lifting a brow and flashing her attitude.

"But you're a year behind me. You can't already be doing fractions. We just barely started them. My daddy told me your schools are way behind ours. He said your brains aren't as big as ours." Betty never meant to sound harsh, but she could tell by the reaction on Alma's face she'd crossed a line.

"When are you going to realize your daddy is a moron?" Alma huffed, and Betty realized how profound that statement was. She wasn't surprised by Alma's opinion of her father but the fact she was willing to say it to her spoke volumes about how she saw Betty as a friend, not someone to fear.

"Everything he's told you so far is malarkey. I'm tired of talking about this stuff. How would you like it if I told you stuff about you that wasn't true? If I walked into your house and plopped myself down and just started saying how dumb you are, how dirty you are? Can't we ever talk about anything different?" Alma pursed her lips and folded her arms across her chest.

Betty gave it some thought. She had been coming here for two weeks and for the most part the only thing they ever talked about was what Betty was interested in. And it did usually turn out to be something that was probably pretty insulting. She had no clue what Alma liked. "What do you want to talk about? Is there anything you like to do?"

"I make bracelets," Alma said proudly, unfolding her arms and turning her wrist out so Betty could see one. Tied tightly and looped around three times was a colorful woven bracelet. "My daddy brings extra thread and string home from the mill, and I turn it into these. I taught myself how to make all different kinds."

"Wow." Betty smiled, leaning in close to see the intricate pattern the different colored threads had created. "Can you teach me how to make one?"

"I can try. It might be hard since our brains are different sizes," Alma teased. "I'll go get my basket of thread." Alma jogged off around the corner and quickly reappeared with a tiny basket and a big smile. Guilt nagged at Betty's stomach at the realization she'd been so painfully rude and selfish since meeting Alma. The world had suddenly gotten so serious around her she forgot what having a little fun felt like.

Within a few minutes the walls between the girls crumbled under the weight of their laughter. Two bracelets and four cookies later they'd made more than something nice to wear on their wrists. They'd built a bridge between them with thread and knots.

"I'm sorry if the stuff I've been asking sounds rude. I didn't mean any of it that way. I'm starting to think everything everyone says about colored folks is pretty much a lie. I just don't understand why. When did all this start?" Betty slipped a bracelet on Alma's wrist and tied it tightly for her.

"I dunno know. A long time ago, I guess. Maybe that's the question you should be asking Mama. She knows all about history and stuff. Her grandma was a slave."

"Where is she anyway? It's almost time for me to get gone before your daddy comes home. Has she ever been this late before?"

"She has to stay after school sometimes. That's probably it." Alma didn't look up from her bracelet as she spoke, and Betty could tell she was fighting worry.

Betty opened her mouth to offer something comforting but stopped when she heard a board on the front porch creak. "Go in the back room," Alma ordered, jumping to her feet to see out the window.

"Don't bother," Winnie's voice called as she pushed open the door. "I heard you two laughing from down the street. And when you tell someone to hide you gotta tell them quiet like. You two were as loud as the choir on Easter Sunday.

"Sorry, Mama," Alma offered as she dove into her mother's arms. "Where have you been? You're so late."

"Was a long day, that's all. Now tell me what you two girls are doing making all that ruckus. The way you've been acting lately I figured I'd come home and you two would be throwing punches at each other, not laughing and playing."

"We made up," Betty said, throwing a smile at Alma. "I was being kind of a pain asking all those questions but never really getting to know you. I'm sorry for that."

"Making bracelets helped," Alma added, showing her mom the matching bracelets they were both wearing.

Winnie looked down at their wrists pressed together, showing off what they'd done like it was a badge of honor. "Look at you two. Look at this right here." She held both their wrists as her eyes began to well with tears. "How come two little girls can figure this out but the whole country can't get it right?"

"Mama, why are you crying? What happened?" Alma's face filled with worry at the sight of her mother's show of emotion.

Winnie moved over toward the table and gestured for them both to sit down. "I've told you a lot over the last couple of weeks. You understand now the difference between what the government is insisting on versus what's actually happening in places like Edenville. But certain things, like segregation of the schools, can't go on anymore. They're cracking down. They're forcing it. I've told you about how it's been in other places. I was hoping they'd keep it at bay a while longer here though."

"Wouldn't you want Alma going to our schools? We have all new books and they just built a whole new music room." Betty cocked her head to the side looking thoroughly confused.

"It's not safe," Winnie sighed, dropping her head down. "She wouldn't be safe there. But it's nothing to fret over because I worked it out. She doesn't have to go."

"I don't? Thank you, Mama. I don't wanna go through all that. I've seen what they do to us. How did you work it out?"

"I promised to teach there instead," Winnie announced, turning her chin up as though it was an unavoidable truth.

"No," Alma cried, her face crumpling. "You can't, Mama. You can't go into that school and try to teach. You know how bad it will be."

"There's nothing we can do about it. It is what it is. I'll start there next quarter, and as long as I do, you won't have to go there. We're nearly out of here anyway. You know that."

Betty's heart skipped a beat at the thought of them leaving. "What do you mean you're nearly out of here? Where are you going?"

"You think we live in squalor for nothing? Every dime we don't spend on fancy things and a decent house has been saved so we can move from this hateful place. Since the day Alma was born we've been just biding our time until we can get somewhere safer. My husband's mama just passed on a few months ago, and she was the last of our kin. We've got nearly enough to leave," Winnie explained, noticeably unable to meet Betty's sad eyes.

"You can't just leave. For weeks you've been telling me all about these people trying to make things better. They're fighting against this and being brave. How can you want to run away? Don't you want to be a fighter?" Betty furrowed her brows as she tried to make a case for her new friends to stay in Edenville.

Winnie's face hardened in a way that made Betty's stomach flip over with anxiety. She did her share of making grown-ups angry, but so far Winnie had been immensely patient with her.

"I am not a fighter because I am a mother first. Do you know what kind of hellfire would rain down over this family if we went and sat at a lunch counter and waited to be served? I won't do that to my child. It's not fair," Winnie shot back angrily. "My job is not to fix the world, it's to keep her safe while it's broken. You are damn lucky you aren't my child right now."

Betty's head drooped and tears filled the corners of her eyes as she realized how badly she'd hurt Winnie.

"She means if you were hers she'd be whooping you right now," Alma interjected but quieted quickly when her mother shot her a look.

"I'm sorry," Betty whispered. "I don't think you're a coward. I just don't want you to leave. I don't want to be here either."

With a huff Winnie stood and opened her arms to Betty who dove into them with force as the tears flowed freely down her face.

Before any of them could speak again footsteps crossed the front porch. Alma sprang forward, but Betty was frozen in fear as the door opened.

Chapter Seven

"Nate you scared us half to death," Winnie sighed as the man dropped his heavy bag and moved toward them. Betty could easily deduce this was Alma's dad. They shared so many features, and she'd heard Winnie use the name Nate when speaking about him before. But that knowledge didn't alleviate her fear. How would they explain away her presence here?

"What are you doing home early, Daddy?" Alma asked as she threw her arms around his waist. Betty watched as his face lit up while holding his daughter. She couldn't remember a time when her father had looked half as pleased to see her.

Betty shrank back, trying to make herself as small as possible, and thought maybe it was working because no one had addressed her yet. Surely she'd be in big trouble for being here, so she readied herself as Nate began to speak. "I got word about the school integrating, and the boss let me take off to come see if you were all right. Everyone was talking about how you were on the short list of teachers. They can't really force you to work there, can they?" Nate asked, running a hand over his wife's cheek, heavy worry on his brow.

"It's me or Alma. That's what they told me," Winnie choked out, looking ready to cry.

"I should get on home," Betty said just above a whisper as she made a move for the door.

"Aren't you gonna say hi to my daddy?" Alma asked, giving Betty a cross look as though she were being terribly rude.

"I-I didn't think he'd want me here," she stammered in a tiny voice as she stared down at her shoes.

"I don't," he said flatly, "but they do, and they always get what they want when it comes to me. I'm a sucker for a few tears." Nate gave a shrug and a half smile.

"You already knew I've been coming here?" Betty asked with wide eyes. She had assumed the moment he found out he'd put an end to it.

"I don't keep secrets from my husband," Winnie said, planting a kiss on his cheek. "I just bother him until he lets me do things my way, like any good marriage."

"But you should get on home," Nate said, his dark eyes soft but tired. Betty was in awe of his height. He towered over her and would have stood a few inches over her father even. His shoulders were wide under his dirty cotton jumpsuit, and she could tell his battered hands had already worked a lifetime. "It's getting wild out there all of a sudden. Word's spreading that at the start of next term there'll be black teachers at Edenville East. People are gathering in the center of Main Street protesting. I doubt it'll end there. That kind of stuff takes on a life of its own at some point."

"I bet my daddy's there," Betty said absent-mindedly, as though she were giving a weather update. "He doesn't think we should be mixing in school or church or anywhere. He's Klan."

"You ain't telling me anything I don't already know. That's why I don't think it's a good idea to have you coming round here. But when Winnie has her mind set to something there ain't no changing it." Nate and Winnie exchanged a knowing look that Betty couldn't read.

"You got that right," Alma snickered.

"Thank you, sir, for letting me come here. I don't have nothing else to look forward to all day." Betty reached for the door handle but froze when Nate grabbed her wrist suddenly.

"You hear that?" he asked in a hushed voice. Betty strained her ears but the only thing she could hear was the nervous thumping of her heart. "There's a crowd coming," he said with a crackling, nervous voice.

Winnie peered out the window, working hard to keep from being seen. "It's a whole mess of people coming down the hill like a swarm of angry bees. You gotta hide, girl."

"No," Nate grunted, dragging Betty toward the side door. "You've got time. You can get up those rocks, but you've gotta go now."

"But what are they doing here? What'll they do to you?" Betty's heart was thudding fiercely when Nate swung open the side door.

"It won't be nothing compared to what they'll be doing if they catch you here. Go on," he said in a hushed voice as he shoved her forward again.

The smell of wet moss overtook Betty's nose as she shimmied herself up the rocks and tucked herself away where she couldn't be seen. It would have been wise of her to run straight home, but something kept her frozen. She couldn't see over the rock she was tucked behind, but she closed her eyes and strained to hear any noise she could. Her labored breathing settled, and she folded her hands together, praying hard for all sorts of things that were bolting through her head. She prayed she wouldn't get caught. She prayed the crowd coursing through the dirt streets that separated the shacks would not hurt anyone.

There were moments she wanted to cover her ears to block out the shouting of obscenities and hatred but she forced herself to listen. This was what Winnie had told her was going on in the world. This is what was happening here, and hearing it herself solidified it for her.

Betty watched the sun fall below the tree line and heard the thundering crowd fall away. She wanted so desperately to go back and make sure Alma and Winnie were safe, but she knew she'd already be in trouble back home for being out past sunset. She stood, peered down quickly at the shack and then ran off into the woods. Whipping branches slapped across her face and thorny thickets latched to her socks as she raced back home.

Her house came into view and her stomach turned with unease. Nothing about coming home ever felt good anymore. The only thing she craved now was the warm fire burning at Winnie's house and a giant heaping of her special mashed potatoes. She'd trade any of her belongings for one tight hug from the woman who made everything feel a little less scary.

Chapter Eight

Betty leaned back in her chair and took a long sip of her bourbon. Every wide eye was fixed on her, and she felt compelled to finish the story even though her heart was aching.

"Were they hurt?" Bobby asked, breaking the silence that had enveloped them all as they sat motionless on the porch waiting to hear more.

"Maybe we should take a break and come back tomorrow to finish the story," Michael suggested, running his eyes over Betty appraisingly. He was usually the one in the crowd who could sense someone's angst. As a lawyer, his time in the courtroom gave him the ability to read a situation before almost anyone else.

"But I want to know what happened. Was Alma hurt? What were those people doing there that night? I don't get it." Frankie's voice was splintered with confusion and worry that sent chills down Betty's spine.

"You don't hear this from me too often, but I think maybe I made a bad judgment call tonight. You might not be old enough yet to hear all this," Betty said, running a hand over Frankie's cheek.

Frankie huffed out her frustration. "You said I'm not much younger than you were while this was happening. I'm just listening to the story. You *lived* it."

"I didn't have a choice. Everything I've told you up until this point is tame compared to where this story goes. I think maybe I made a mistake. You don't even need to know this darkness exists."

"I want to hear," Frankie insisted, folding her arms across her chest defiantly. "You wouldn't leave Winnie's kitchen when you wanted her to tell you all about the world. She tried to tell you to go and you didn't. Everyone tells me all the time how much I'm like you. I won't leave either."

"I know I'm supposed to scold here, but as a lawyer I'm impressed with her argument," Michael interjected as he dodged a glare from Betty and a slap to the ribs from Jules.

"She does have a point," Piper added. "There's no one on this porch more like you than Frankie. I think it's important for her to hear what it was like for you back then."

Betty downed the last sip of amber liquid in her glass and groaned. "Piper and Michael, you're the biggest troublemakers. I feel like we should just get that out now. When you two are together I always know I'll be dealing with nonsense. But let's hear what her mama thinks about it."

Jules shifted in her seat, her eyes darting between a pathetically pleading Frankie and everyone else on the porch. "It's a part of Edenville's history. It happened. Whether she learns about it on this porch or out in the world, she'll hear it eventually. I'd rather have her here where she can ask questions and understand what that time was really like."

"Good," Frankie said victoriously but toned it down instantly when her mother shot her a look of warning.

"Do any of y'all have any questions for me?" Betty asked, holding her glass out so Clay could refill it.

"I do," Piper interjected. "The first time I sat at your table you told me your recipes were handed down from past generations, and your mother was the first person to put sour cream in her potatoes. But you just said Winnie taught you to make her special potatoes."

"I'll never take away the fact that my folks gave me life. They brought me into the world, and I truly believe they did the best they knew how. But when I close my eyes and think about a mama I think of Winnie. That's where I learned to cook. That's where I learned how to be a person, a real human being. There's a big difference between a mother and a mama. Those recipes, the ones I said were handed down . . . they were Winnie's."

"How did you get to be nearly a teenager and still not know what was going on in the world?" Jules asked. "It was such a tumultuous time throughout the country, but you didn't seem to realize it."

"I sure didn't know what the hell was happening. Edenville was very insulated and my household even more so. We didn't have a television, and my parents could hardly read, so we weren't much for sitting around with the paper. Once I started to learn more about it from Winnie, things I'd heard in the past started to make sense. I guess I just didn't know people had that capacity to hate each other. But once I knew, there was no turning back."

"I thought the Supreme Court ruled on segregation in the late fifties. You're talking about four or five years later." Bobby shook his head as though the entire idea of the history of Edenville made him feel ill.

"I don't know the legal mumbo jumbo of it all. I just know Edenville held out until they couldn't anymore. But that night the people stormed through what was known as the west side shacks and wreaked havoc. They made it clear while the courts had ruled it illegal to keep blacks out of their white school, they weren't going to swing their doors open and give a warm welcome."

"People must've been so scared back then," Frankie remarked quietly as she squeezed in tighter to her mom.

"I can't imagine having to sit in our house while a bunch of angry people came shouting at us for something we didn't even do. You wouldn't let that happen would you, Daddy?" Her eyes were wide and begging for Michael to assure her he'd always be there to protect her.

He stopped short of a blind assurance made just for the sake of comforting her. Betty knew Michael to be rooted in reality, and his answer was no surprise. "You never know what the world is going to bring, but that's why I work so hard. The law is there to protect us and make sure things like that never happen again." He reached his arm over and pulled Frankie tight to him.

Frankie's worries were still not warmly tucked away as her eyes danced between the adults. "What about the police? Where were they that night? Couldn't Winnie have just called them? Uncle Bobby wouldn't let something like that go on," she reasoned, the wheels in her head clearly spinning to make sense of something Betty knew couldn't be figured out by anyone.

"You're damn right I wouldn't have let that go on," Bobby shot back, looking as though his anger was growing by the minute. "It's a disgrace how long this went on here. That it ever happened at all. You'd think this was hundreds of years ago, but it's not. It's within your lifetime, Betty. It pisses me off."

"Back then," Betty started, softening her face as not to bring about any useless anger that wouldn't do anyone any good, "if a white man did something bad, even killed a black man, he rarely went to prison for it. If the police were around they either joined right in or looked the other way. The police were there for us, not for them."

"You sure you want to go on with your story?" Clay asked, lacing his fingers with Betty's as her voice grew more agitated.

"Telling it won't change the outcome. It won't heal all the hurt, but at least y'all will know the people who shaped me."

"And we want to know that, Mama," Jules said earnestly. "I've never asked before. I could always tell you didn't want to talk about the letters from Alma. You didn't want me to know about all the hurt that happened to you, so I'm glad to be hearing it now. I've always wanted to know."

"Well I guess I can't argue with all these big eyes and gaped mouths staring at me. If you want to know the ugly truth of it all, then I'll tell you. That night Winnie, Nate, and Alma did not escape the mob of angry people, and it was a good thing Nate turned me out when he did, otherwise it would have been much worse."

Chapter Nine

Edenville 1961

Coming home late on a night when such big news had broken did earn Betty a few slaps on her way up to bed though her mother did look relieved to see she was not harmed in all the commotion in town. As usual when sent to bed, she camped out at the top of the stairs and listened hard to hear all her parents had to say.

"It's slipping away," her father snarled. "Everything we've been doing is breaking up and falling apart. They're letting five Negro teachers come into the school and teach our kids. It's sinful." There was a loud thud Betty recognized as her father's hand slamming down on their large oak table.

"Can't you do nothing? The Klan isn't planning anything? I don't want our daughter getting taught by some idiot," her mother answered in a shrill and worried voice.

"You're the idiot," Betty whispered and then quickly repented and did the sign of the cross twice. Little did her mother know, even though she hadn't started working at Edenville East yet, Winnie was already teaching Betty. She'd learned more in the last two weeks than she had in all the years leading up to it. From current events to the perfect buttermilk biscuit recipe, her brain was more full than it had ever been before. So was her heart.

Betty tried her best, but three days of staying away from Alma's house was all she could manage. The more talk that circled the town, the more she needed to see her friends. The first chance she had to slip away she took it.

"Not today, Betty," was all Winnie said through the door. "It's not safe."

Betty wanted to sit there in protest but the truth in Winnie's words couldn't be ignored. The whole world felt unsafe now. Betty could see the burned out shacks just around the corner from Winnie's. There was a noose hanging from the tree at the foot of the hill Betty ran down to get to them. Hate had touched the place Betty had imagined was protected by love. She turned away from Winnie's porch and drudged back to the woods. Shacks that weren't burned were covered in spray paint, curse words and hateful things marked on every available surface. If the people who did this understood how kind everyone here was then surely they'd stop. Betty considered parading down Main Street and educating everyone. But now, thanks to Winnie, she knew better.

When she turned on her heel to leave she prayed things would go back to the way they were before. If only she could keep coming to Alma's and making bracelets and learning to cook. The world wouldn't be perfect, she understood that, but her little piece of it could be good.

She could still smell the smoke of Winnie's cooking fire when she saw him. About ten yards to the left of the path to her home was a person wobbling without much sense of direction. Looking more like an animal than a man, the sight of him made her heart stiffen with fear.

Betty crouched down and held her breath until she could get a better look at the figure moving toward her. The tightness in her chest faded away instantly when she saw the familiar face.

"Simpson," she shouted as she shot up to a standing position. "What are you doing out here?"

"Beatrice?" he asked, seeming to look through her rather than at her. "What are you . . .?" his voice trailed off as he swayed on his feet.

The closer he got the more Betty could tell what was wrong. Simpson's eyes were rimmed purple and the skin of his brow was split open. Slumping shoulders and a limp in his step let Betty know he'd been beaten up. One of his hands was pressing tight to a rag on his other wrist.

"What happened to you?" Betty asked, running up to help steady him. He stood six inches taller than her and during the last summer his shoulders had filled out. She'd have no real shot of holding him up if his legs gave out completely, but she had to try.

"I pissed off my jerk of a dad again," he grumbled as he leaned himself against a tree. "Get out of here. Leave me alone."

"I can't leave you here. Your arm is bleeding. If I go get help you might pass out, stop putting pressure on your arm, and bleed to death. And there's no way I can get you all the way back home by myself." Betty's mind was racing through her options. Simpson had been a pain in the ass over the years but she'd also known him since they were babies. No matter how much of a jerk he'd tried to be, every single time it came down to helping her, he always did. She wanted to repay the kindness he'd always tried to pretend he wasn't giving her.

"Leave me alone. I don't want anyone's help." With a halfhearted swat of his hand, Simpson tried to shoo her away. In doing so he exposed the cut that was spurting blood from his wrist.

"Cover it," Betty shouted, grabbing the rag and using her hand to press down on his wound. "Come on, I know where we can go."

Simpson opened his mouth to protest but no words came. His eyes fixated on Betty's tiny fingers clutched around his wrist. When his mouth clamped shut again she grabbed the collar of his shirt with her free hand and yanked him along.

At the top of the hill at the edge of the woods she looked down over Winnie's house and then back at Simpson. This was a terrible idea. No one would be pleased with her. Surely she'd lose more than one friend by the time the sun set this evening. But at least no one would die.

"Who lives there?" Simpson asked as he tripped his way down the hill toward the shack.

"They're my friends. They'll help you," Betty explained, praying she was right about both those statements.

Simpson tried to pull away but it only made him less steady. "We can't, Beatrice."

"Don't call me that. Round here they call me Betty. You best do the same. Now you can either stay up in those woods and die, or you can let them help you."

Rather than knocking on the door, Betty pushed her way right in and shoved Simpson into a kitchen chair as Winnie came barreling around the corner. "Betty, what in God's name are you doing here? And who is this?"

"His name's Simpson. He's my friend, and he's hurt bad. He'll bleed to death unless we fix up his arm. I couldn't get him all the way back home, and I didn't know what else to do. You ain't gonna turn us out like this are you?" Betty made her face fierce and determined as Winnie's eyes danced between her and Simpson.

"You're gonna be the death of me, child," Winnie sighed. "Alma, come on out here. You need to fetch Cynthia. Tell her there's a boy here who needs stiches."

When Alma rounded the corner she gasped and hid behind her mother. "That's the boy who chased me with the bat," she cried, clutching her mother's apron.

"He's hurt bad," Betty argued. "He doesn't have a bat now. He couldn't do anything to you. He can barely stand."

Winnie reached a hand back to comfort Alma who was shaking with fear. "You brought the boy who tried to hurt my daughter into my house, Betty? In what world does that sound like something you should do?"

"In the world where we don't let people die alone in the woods. Simpson told us where the other boys were that day and gave us a chance to run. He saved us both, really." Betty looked down at Simpson, whose color was fading away, and implored him with angry eyes to speak up.

"I wasn't gonna hit you. I saw you there, and I chased you in a different direction away from the group I was with. I was trying to get you back over to this side of town before they had a chance to catch up. You don't want to know what would've happened if you crossed their path." Simpson's words came slowly as he tried to muster his strength. "I couldn't hit no little girl with a bat. There's a lot I can't do, just ask my pa. He'll tell you. It's why he beat me like this."

"My great grandmamma used to say the way people treat their kids is a reflection of how they feel about themselves," Winnie offered, as she seemed to give the boy more thought.

"If that's true my daddy hates himself," Simpson muttered.

"Go on and get Cynthia," Winnie insisted as she shook Alma off her and shoved her toward the door. "Tell her to come alone."

"But Mama," Alma protested angrily.

"He'll be the least of your worries if you disobey me right now. Go on," Winnie snapped, raising a threatening brow at her daughter.

Betty used her free hand to tilt Simpson's head back and examine the cut over his eye. "Why'd you come all this way through the woods? Why not just go to Dr. Peters? You know he'd have fixed you up."

"I just wanted to go out in the woods and walk and lie down." Simpson closed his eyes and bit at his bloody lip.

"That ain't no plan. Lie down and what?" Betty asked, assuming he must have some kind of brain damage to be talking so dumb.

Simpson's stare was blank and unemotional as he explained. "Lie down and die. I just wanted to walk where no one would be looking for me and put my head on a pile of leaves and sleep forever."

"Simpson, that's stupid. Why would you wanna die?" Betty let go of his arm and moved her hands angrily but remembered quickly the blood squirting from his wrist.

"Pull some clean towels in from the clothes line," Winnie ordered as she used her hip to bump Betty aside. She gripped the towel and held it in place, putting pressure on it.

Betty hustled outside, yanked the towels from the line, and bolted back through the door. She didn't want to be seen outside, and she didn't want to miss Simpson's explanation, because as far as she was concerned there couldn't be one.

"I'm gonna die anyway," Simpson proclaimed, staring Winnie dead in the eye. "That's how it is now. I'm either with them, or I'm against them, and if I'm against them, I'm dead. I wanted to go out on my terms, not dragged behind some car or hung from a damn tree. You can understand that, can't you?"

Betty heard his words but they didn't compute. The only way she could tell for sure what he was saying was profound was by the look on Winnie's face. Her jaw was clenched tight and her nostrils flared, and Betty couldn't tell if Winnie was angry or just overwhelmed.

"What'd you cut yourself with?" Winnie asked, matching his fierce stare. Betty felt as though she was watching two gladiators about to face off.

"His daddy beat him," Betty chimed in, assuming she was helping, but it was as if she'd suddenly become invisible. Neither of them even blinked at the sound of her voice.

"Pocket knife," Simpson answered flatly. "It was too dull I think. It didn't quite do the job."

"The job?" Betty asked, tossing her hands up as though they were all speaking another language now.

"What'd he want you to do that was so bad you were willing to end it all?" Winnie took the clean rags from Betty's hand and wrapped his wound tightly.

"A few days ago they all come down here hooting and hollering. They were trying to scare y'all off from coming to our school. I told him I'd be here. I was just going to go into town and round up a few more boys like he asked. I never showed up. I told him I got hung up messing with this kid from the west side that wandered over to our farm. One of my brothers ratted me out though and told my pa I was in town laying low."

"Whatcha gonna do?" Winnie asked, as though the topic didn't weigh a thousand pounds. As if there was some kind of simple answer. "I'm not gonna let you die here, so what's your plan then?"

"I just wanted to hang on a couple more years. I'll be fourteen at the end of this year. I can get a job, sock some cash away, and get out of here. Nothing's ever gonna change here, and if I stay the only thing I can ever be is like my pa or dead. Now I can see I don't have a couple years, there ain't no such thing as too young anymore. We're all supposed to take up the fight. We're all supposed to be soldiers."

"Can't you just stay out the way? That's what I'm doing," Betty interjected, peeking out the window to see if Alma was on her way back yet.

"It don't work like that for me. I tried."

Winnie still seemed to have an air of skepticism as she probed Simpson for more. "You've been hearing the same junk over and over again since you were little, I'm sure. What makes you any different than your pa? I wouldn't think you'd know any better."

"I got eyes and a brain of my own. Look at this right here," Simpson grunted back defensively, gesturing around the room with his uninjured hand. "You know what woulda happened if this had been the other way around? You think any of my kin would have fetched help for your daughter if she were hurt? They'd probably've been the ones to hurt her in the first place. I read the newspapers. I see what's going on in the world.

I've known for years my family wasn't on the right side of this."

Winnie nodded her head but didn't say another word. They waited in silence until Cynthia, a trained nurse, came charging through the door with a small satchel over her shoulder. Her short black hair was pulled back in rollers as if she'd been pulled out of bed.

"What the hell?" she asked, freezing so quickly when she saw Simpson that Alma slammed into her back. "You wake me up in the middle of the day, knowing I've worked all night, for *this*?"

"His wrist is cut. He needs some stiches," Winnie directed, the sternness in her face not leaving any room for debate.

"It seems like he should have a doctor of his own to help him. This here is Merle's boy. If he don't like the way I stitch him up, what's he gonna do to me?" Cynthia's halfhearted protest didn't stop her from opening up her bag and taking a seat next to Simpson.

"I'm not gonna say anything to anyone about being here if none of you will," Simpson assured them.

Cynthia worked in silence, numbed the area, and began closing his wound. She wrapped bright white gauze around his arm and then began checking his other injuries. "You may have a broken rib," she reported as he winced under the pressure of her touch. "You should be seen by a doctor."

Simpson grunted unconvincingly as he buttoned his blood-stained shirt. Trying to get himself more upright in the rickety wooden chair, he yelped in pain. "I'm fine," he choked out as he waved them all off. "I just need a minute, and I'll be out of here."

"You lost a good amount of blood. You can't be walking home. You need to rest and get your strength back." Cynthia packed up her small bag and headed for the door. "Winnie, I hope you know what you're doing here. I'd do just about anything for you. Most everyone round here would. Just be sure you aren't asking us to do something that's gonna get us killed."

As Cynthia slipped out the door, the room was taken over by an awkward silence. Alma and Betty moved over toward the table and sat down, all four of the wobbly chairs occupied now.

"I'll fix y'all something to eat. You like okra?" Winnie asked. "Alma, fetch something out of the medicine cabinet for the boy's pain."

"You don't need to cook me nothing. You've done enough already. Your friend is right, me being here ain't no good for anyone. Me and Betty'll be on our way." Simpson grunted as he shifted in the chair.

"Being here is good for me," Betty argued, starting out timidly and then gaining more confidence. "When I'm here no one is calling me names. No one's pushing me around. Winnie, Nate, and Alma treat me more like kin than my own folks do. And I help out round here too."

"How lucky for you," Simpson huffed. "Don't you ever think about what it means for them? You can't be hanging round here. Nobody's gonna give a rat's ass why when they come stringing up her daddy for having you here."

"Ain't nobody gonna string up my daddy. He'll kill your daddy before he lets that happen," Alma shouted, shooting up from the table.

"Shut up, all y'all. I can't tell you what you're supposed to do out there. I don't have an answer, but I can tell you in here, in this house, you will treat each other with kindness. There might be wild animals banging down this door, but if you step over this threshold you won't act like them. Now sit down, and find a way to get on with each other while I fix the food. Simpson isn't going anywhere until he's had something to eat, so work it out."

"I don't have nothing to say to him," Alma snapped as she turned her back to him.

"You better use your proper English, child. I don't stay up late nights teaching you just so you can sound like a fool. If you don't have *anything* to say to him then sit down and listen. Why do you think God gave you a mouth that could close but ears that couldn't?"

"Yes, Mama," Alma said before closing her lips exactly the way God intended her to.

"I've learned a lot coming here, Simpson," Betty said in a tiny voice, still unsure of the odd dynamic between this mismatched trio.

"Like what?" he asked skeptically.

"I've heard all about the sit-ins and the Freedom Riders. All sorts of stuff they won't teach us in school." Betty beamed with pride at how knowledgeable she was now about the world.

"Speaking of school, you'll be teaching there next quarter won't ya?" Simpson asked, leaning slightly to catch Winnie's reaction as she bustled around the kitchen.

"Looks like it," Winnie replied as though she didn't have time for the conversation.

"That's really brave," he said, clearly thinking he was paying her a compliment.

"Brave? You think I knocked on their door and demanded a spot? You think I'm going because I want to change the world? I'll be teaching there because I made a deal to keep Alma out of that school in exchange for my unwelcomed services. That's not brave. If I signed up to go there on my own that would be like making my own storm then complaining when I get struck by lightning." Winnie stoked the fire and brought the oven to life with a roar of ash and smoke.

"It don't matter how they got you there, if you show up then it's brave." Simpson shimmied to the edge of the chair and tried to stand but lost his balance and flopped back down.

"You eat," Winnie ordered, pointing her wooden mixing spoon at the boy. "Just sit right there and eat."

It wasn't long before the table was covered with food. Too early to be dinner, too big to be an after-school snack, the three kids partook happily in the impromptu meal. And as it sometimes did, food closed the gap between them all. Laughter erupted when they compared notes about the three-legged goat at the farm adjacent to the woods. Silly names and puns had their sides splitting as they passed plates of food to one another.

Two hours ticked by, and Betty watched Winnie frequently peer out the window to make sure no one was coming. She wondered who Winnie feared might show up.

The color had returned to Simpson's cheeks, and he seemed to doing much better by the minute.

"Looks like food did the trick," Winnie smiled as she stacked their plates and carted them toward the sink.

84

"Thanks," Simpson said as he grabbed his hat and plopped it back on his head. "I'll make sure no one's looking, and me and Betty'll get out of here."

"Wait," Alma cried as she darted out of the room, leaving them all to worry that something was wrong. When she scurried back in she held a bracelet in her hand. "Me and Betty wear these. It's like we're secret friends and these bracelets mean something to us. You want one?" Even though Betty wasn't very experienced out in the world, she could tell Alma was holding more than just a bracelet in her extended hand. It was an olive branch. It was her heart.

"I can't wear that. I can't be friends with you, and you know why," Simpson huffed.

Alma's eyes dropped to the ground, and she stared at her shoes. "I didn't think you were like that."

"Well I am. There ain't no way I'm gonna be friends with a couple of girls." Simpson's deadpan look cracked away and was replaced by a hyena laugh. When the girls realized his joke they started laughing too. Alma ignored his words, and grabbed his uninjured wrist, and slipped the bracelet on.

"Gross, cooties," Simpson joked, and they all broke down in tear-inducing laughter again. Alma tightened the knot on his bracelet just as the door to the shack swung open.

Nate stood there, looking nervous at first as the laughter died down. He surveyed the scene, watching this white boy's hand in his daughter's as they giggled at some joke he'd missed.

For the first time since she'd started coming here, Betty watched Winnie's expression change to a guilty embarrassment.

They all stood in a stony silence until Nate finally chiseled his way through it.

"For goodness sake Winnie—call the newspapers. They're multiplying."

Chapter Ten

Two weeks later they'd all found a way to make it work. For the kids it was a relief, but Betty could tell, for Winnie and Nate, the weight of the world was on their shoulders.

"We always said for Alma's sake we wouldn't be sticking our noses into the problems of the world," Nate murmured to Winnie as they sat on their front porch. They were swinging away on the swing Nate had made out of pallets from the factory. Their hushed voices should have been quiet enough to go unheard by the three kids in the house, but still Betty managed to eavesdrop.

Alma and Simpson were sitting at the wobbly table playing cards as Betty carried all their plates filled with cookie crumbs to the sink. She lingered there to hear what Winnie and Nate were talking about.

"We have to balance the need to protect Alma with our responsibility to show her compassion and empathy. I'm sorry this is hard on you, but I just see these kids and can't imagine locking them out." Winnie shrugged and shot him a look.

"What is it you always say to Alma? It's better to stop the apology before you get to the part with the excuse," Nate crowed back, not able to hold the smile from forming.

"Don't go putting my own wisdom back on me. That's against the rules. Plus it's not like I'm carrying a damn sign or sitting at the counter of the dime store demanding a milk shake," Winnie defended.

"No, you're babysitting a couple white kids right here in our house. Best-case scenario: you're going to end up with a disappointed and broken heart. Trying to protect these kids in a world like ours is like trying to plant seeds in the dead of winter. Even if you manage to break through the frozen earth, nothing can come of it. You can't grow flowers in the snow." Nate's voice wasn't angry; it was sympathetic and pleading.

Winnie shook her head solemnly as his words seemed to strike at her very heart. "Then you turn them out. Send them back to their miserable parents so they can get beaten some more. If you think it's the right thing to do, then you do it. I won't stop you."

"I will," Nate said firmly. "Tomorrow maybe." Betty couldn't interpret the look they exchanged. It might have been a knowing and understanding look or a serious one. She backed away from the window and headed somberly over to the table.

"I think your daddy is finally gonna turn us out of here tomorrow and tell us not to come back," she reported sadly as she took her seat.

Alma snickered and rolled her eyes. "I'm pretty sure he says that every night. But Mama does sound serious about you guys not hanging around here after school starts. She just can't risk it. Best I can tell, that's really the end for us all being here together."

"So we need another place," Betty determined as she waited for Simpson to deal her in.

"There is no other place," Simpson cut back. His words were sharp but his face was soft with disappointment. Betty loved coming to Alma's but Simpson seemed to need it even more than she did. "Tell her, Alma. Once your mama says it's done then it's done."

"I'm not ready to quit hanging around with you guys," Alma whispered. "Maybe if we all think about it we can come up with a place where we can meet up after school. We need it to be like a club just for us."

"Don't be dumb," Simpson grumbled. "We're not babies. We can't just make up some club and think that'll be a real thing. It'll be a lot harder than that."

"It's funny, you don't say ain't as much anymore. My mama's got you talking proper." Alma picked up her cards from the table and hid her face behind them.

"Stop screwing around, you two," Betty snapped sternly. "We need to find a way to be able to see each other after Winnie starts teaching. Simpson, you know the woods best. You know where all the worst boys in town hang out. We can stay clear of there."

Simpson shook his head as he laid down his first card and thought it over. "There's only one place those guys don't go. Bill Napter's land is pretty much off limits. He's crazier than a bag of weasels, and I can't think of a kid who would step a toe on his land. It's mostly just old stories about the guy that probably are not even true. He's got tons of barns and sheds I bet he's forgotten about."

"And what, we're just going to go there and play cards after school? If everyone else is too scared to go there then why wouldn't we be?" Alma plopped her cards down and made it clear she wasn't feeling much like playing anymore.

"The rest of town is scarier to me than that place," Simpson admitted. I can bring some supplies. Food. Lanterns. Even some fold-out chairs. We could find one of his old sheds that isn't too rundown and make it nice. The guy is almost eighty, it's not like he leaves the house much anymore. We'll be fine." Simpson gestured for Alma to pick up her cards and play, but she still hesitated.

"And if he does find us?" she asked, raising her brows nearly to her hairline.

Simpson straightened his shoulders and tried to look bigger than he was. "I can handle him."

"So are we doing this?" Betty asked, looking hopeful for the first time since they'd sat down.

"Doing what?" Winnie asked with a frown as she pushed her way through the door and eyed them all suspiciously.

"Nothing," Alma replied too quickly for her mother's liking. She scooped her cards off the table and started to play again.

Winnie shook her head and tossed her dishtowel over her shoulder. "Well that was wholly unconvincing. Whatever you're scheming, get it out of your heads. I know it isn't fair or fun to have to say goodbye, but you never know what the future holds. Things will settle down here eventually."

"You believe that?" Simpson asked, craning his neck to see Winnie's face.

"I said it, didn't I? By now you should know I don't go around wasting my breath on things I don't believe. Now take a break from that game. Simpson, grab some logs from the back porch to stoke this fire, and girls come help me get the beans made."

"I feel like I could be a chef some day," Betty said, jumping with excitement toward the stove. Cooking was starting to come naturally to her in a way other skills never did.

"You do have a talent for it." Winnie smiled as she handed Betty a large pot. "That could be something to work toward."

"Maybe I'll own my own restaurant some day. When I do I'll let everyone eat there. No matter what they look like. And if people don't like that then they can just shove off." Betty stuck up her chin assertively as though she were already turning away ignorant patrons.

Winnie smiled down lovingly at Betty. "Don't get too big for those tiny little britches. Owning a restaurant is no small thing. You need to know more than just some recipes. You need to understand how to run a business. You need to work on that math you're struggling with."

"I bet you could be good at it, Betty," Simpson said as he slipped his boots back on. "I think we've all got a lot of potential to be something great."

"That's very deep," Alma grinned and batted her lashes affectionately.

"Deep?" Betty chuckled. "I don't think that's something I'd ever call Simpson. I've jumped in mud puddles deeper than him."

"I just mean it sounded real nice," Alma cut back. "A fancy thing to say about our potential."

"Fancy? There is nothing fancy about him. The other day I saw him use a rusty nail to pick a splinter out of his finger. He holds his pants up with a piece of rope when his belt breaks. He doesn't even know how to set a proper table the way you showed us, Winnie. He couldn't remember where the forks go."

"Manners, Betty!" Winnie scolded. "I swear some days I'm not sure you have any."

"You've been teaching me manners all along. I know all about how to eat at a fancy table. I know how to lay my napkin the right way across my lap. I got loads of manners. I'm fancier than he is," Betty defended, feeling threatened. She and Simpson had ragged on each other forever, and occasionally it cut too deep. Winnie was always telling them if no one else was going to be nice to them they might as well be nice to each other.

"Those aren't manners," Winnie explained impatiently. "That's etiquette. A trained monkey can learn etiquette. Manners are not about knowing which fork to use at a table; they're about not pointing out that the person next to you doesn't know something. I get that teasing each other is a normal thing, but I don't want you to miss the message. Calling someone out doesn't make him look bad, it makes you look bad. Remember that."

"Yes ma'am," Betty gulped, feeling badly for what she'd said. The lessons from Winnie were fast-paced, and she didn't mince words, but she was always right. "I hope I end up in your class once you start teaching. I bet you can teach me more than any of the cranky old coots there who hate me." Betty strained the beans that had been soaking overnight and rinsed them in the basin on the counter. She had this vision of Winnie at the head of her class, standing in the sturdy way she always did. Finally Betty would get called on again. Finally she'd be treated like every other student in the class. Maybe even better.

"Don't count on it," Simpson said as he put another small log on the fire. "No offense, Winnie, but I'm not sure they'll even let you in the door unless the President gets the National Guard here. I'm hearing some grumbling about their plans."

"I don't want to talk about it anymore," Alma said with a shudder, fighting tears. "It's still a couple weeks off. I don't want to think about it now."

Nate crossed the threshold to the house and forced a smile. "I hope if you hear anything in particular, boy, you'll tell us. There ain't much we can do but we can be prepared at least."

"That's the thing," Simpson said, staring into the fire. He seemed unable to meet Nate's eye.

"Don't put that on him, Nate," Winnie said, rushing to his defense. "He's just a boy."

"And you're my wife. If he hears they're gonna do something to you I want to know about it. We've let him come here, we treat him good; that's the least he can do," Nate's voice snapped with an edge through the silent house.

"There's something I wanna tell you," Simpson admitted, still not turning away from the now roaring fire. His face glowed with an orange hue as he tried to find the words. "Tonight, I'm supposed to . . ." he trailed off and then puffed up his chest so he could try again. "My daddy told me it's time for me to go to his meeting tonight. He's pissed about me not showing up when they came down here to hassle you guys. I'm supposed to get my hood tonight. I don't know what to do."

"You know exactly what to do," Winnie interrupted, smacking her spatula down on the counter with a thwack. "You are a boy; he is your daddy. You do what he tells you to. If you've got to go to a meeting tonight, if they get you all set up to be one of them, then you do it. You know what they'll do to you if you don't."

"I don't want to," Simpson said, sounding like a child. Over last summer he'd grown into the body of a teenager, but he was still lost somewhere in the limbo between little boy and man. "It's just in my blood. It's not like I'm some kid whose dad just works at the bank. This has been in my family for generations in one way or another."

"What a family heirloom," Nate jeered gruffly.

"I don't want to do it," Simpson pleaded, finally turning around and imploring them to help.

The room went deathly silent. Betty felt the knot in her stomach pull tight as she watched her friend battle something she couldn't even imagine.

"You stop that now," Winnie insisted, going back to work on the pork for the beans. "You do what your daddy tells you to until you're old enough to do something different. You're a boy. When you're a man you can do different if you still want to."

"How can you say that? Knowing what they are all about, how can you tell me to be with them instead of you?" Simpson demanded with a bite of anger.

"I don't make the rules, Simpson. I don't tell people who to be, or what to do with their kids. You're both welcome here a couple more weeks until I start teaching at school. That's what we all agreed to. I'm sorry it's not fair." Winnie forcefully began beating the pork down with a mallet to tenderize it and possibly get out the pain she felt about the world these kids were living in.

"We should get going, Betty," Simpson said, wiping a sniffle away from his nose. "It's getting late. I'll walk you to the edge of your road."

"It'll work out," Nate promised, patting Simpson on the shoulder as he headed out the door. "Keep your head up, boy. You'll figure it out."

Even to Betty, who wasn't faced with the same kind of hardship, Nate's words felt hollow.

The walk home with Simpson was silent, mostly because she couldn't think of a single thing to say that would make him feel better. There was no answer.

"Good luck tonight," Betty said as he waved her off at the edge of the woods by her house. "Sorry, that sounded dumb."

"It did," he agreed. "But thanks. I might have an idea to get out of this stuff anyway. My younger brother told me about a job at a farm here. Maybe I can just stay busy enough to be forgotten about. Even with that, we need to find a place we can still hang out after school. They can make us do whatever they want during the day and even at night, but we need to have a place where we can be the bosses in between. We need a place where we make the rules."

Betty wanted to make him feel better. He was like a brother to her and, as an only child, it made her unsure if a hug was the right thing. Then she remembered Winnie's words ringing in her ear. *Sometimes a hug is the only way to squeeze someone's worry away.*

She leaned in and wrapped her arms around his waist. He flinched, and she could feel him holding his breath as she squeezed him. "You're real brave, Simpson," she gushed into his shoulder.

"Thanks," he muttered, raising his arms and patting her back awkwardly. They both seemed to jump back at the same time, eyes darting away. Before Winnie, hugs had never been a part of either of their lives. It was not something that came naturally. It was taught, and they were finally learning the power of caring about someone more than themselves. What an impossibly hard lesson it was.

Chapter Eleven

"This place is creepy," Alma said, holding the lantern in her shaking hand as they made their way through the cobweb-covered old shed.

"This place is perfect," Simpson countered with wide excited eyes. "He'll never come this far out onto his property, and you can tell no one has been in this place in years. It's sturdy; we can keep it warm though the winter even."

"I'm with Alma. This place is pretty scary. It gives me the heebie-jeebies. What are we even going to do out here?" Betty leaned in close to Alma and slipped her arm around her.

"Whatever we want. We can play cards, read comic books, and I'll even play stupid jacks with you guys if you want. No matter what else is going on out there, we can be here. We just need to clean it up." Simpson started clearing out the center of the small shed. "Look, there's even a bench and a table," he announced as though he'd just found gold at the end of a rainbow.

"It's falling apart," Alma countered with a twisted face.

"I'll fix it. I'll make it all perfect in here. You'll see, and when you do, I'll make you eat crow. You'll love it." Simpson looked around the room as though he could envision it finished. "Just give me some time, and I'll change your minds."

* * * *

To his credit, Betty was shocked to see how the place transformed from a creepy horror movie setting to a clubhouse. Over the course of a week Simpson repaired the table and bench. He cleaned and swept the place. It was impossible to count how many trips he'd made from town out here to get it all done.

"So was I right or what?" Simpson gloated as he spun around the room. "I'm gonna run back to my house real quick and grab the cards. I forgot them. You guys stay put." Simpson jogged out toward the woods and left Betty and Alma to look around some more.

"He did do pretty good," Alma admitted as she sat down on the bench and tapped her fingers on the now level table.

"Can you believe we went from him chasing you with a bat to this? It makes me think that anything can happen. Maybe all this stuff will work out." Betty slid onto the bench next to Alma and tapped a similar beat.

"I'm glad he's our friend," Alma admitted, "even if we can't all go around together out there. I like him." She glanced up to the ceiling and bit at her lip as though she'd regretted her words.

"Wait, you like him, like him?" Betty asked, spinning around quickly to face her embarrassed friend.

"I didn't say that," Alma shouted back.

"You didn't say that, but your face did. He's practically three years older than you." Betty grabbed Alma's arm to try to force her to tell her more.

"Forget it," Alma said shrugging her off. "Don't you dare say anything to him. Don't you dare."

"Promise," Betty said, crossing her finger over her heart. "I knew already though. I could tell by the way you make goggley eyes at him. You stick up for him all the time too."

A thud sent the tiny half-hinged door flying open, and Betty nearly tumbled backward off the bench.

"Ain't this cozy," Nicky, Simpson's older brother, said with his hands balled into fists.

"Nicky," Betty shouted covering her heart with her hand. "You scared me half to death." He was an ugly and bigger version of Simpson. He had the same dark hair and big brown eyes, but his face was covered in acne scars and his teeth were too big for his mouth. One of his eyes always drifted off the wrong way, and it made Betty unsure of where he was looking sometimes. For the most part she steered clear of him whenever she could. Obviously today she couldn't.

"Oh I'm sure you and your little tar-baby friend weren't expecting no company. But now that I'm here, I think I'll join the party." Nicky waggled his brows and smiled a devilish grin.

"We aren't bothering anybody. Just go on." Betty tried to sound confident but the rattle in her voice gave her away. It was nothing compared to the tremble she felt coming from Alma's body pressed against her.

"I'm not going anywhere. And neither are you two. You really don't get it, do you? The world is changing. Sympathizers like you are getting your due. Edenville isn't gonna go down like all those other pussy towns. We're gonna fight. And the fight starts here." Nicky moved a step closer and Betty automatically turned her body to block Alma.

"She's a kid, let her go home. Take your fight up with me," Betty demanded, but Alma squeezed her hand tightly under the table as if she wouldn't leave her friend behind. There wasn't even a full year between the two of them, but Betty had come to feel like her older sister.

"When I tell you to run, you do," Betty whispered to a terrified Alma, whose eyes had widened to the point of nearly popping out of her head.

"Nicky," Simpson said, looking confused as he stepped back into the shed. They all froze for a moment as Nicky tried to work out what his brother would be doing here, and Simpson did the same.

"I told you, where there's one there's always another right behind," Betty hissed, making knowing eyes at Simpson while Nicky looked away. "Now we've got two here to deal with."

"What are you doing out here, Nicky?" Simpson asked again, swallowing hard.

"What are you doing?" Nicky demanded, looking thoroughly suspicious.

"I saw your tracks heading this way, and I followed you. I figured maybe you were up to something, and I wanted in," Simpson improvised, regaining control of his coursing fear. "You hanging out with these girls?" Simpson asked, and Betty nearly grinned at the way he'd turned the tables on his brother.

"Hell no. I was following a bunch of tracks too and came up on this place. This tar-baby and this moron are hiding out here, trying to be friends. But I was just about to break up the party. Now you can help."

"That's Reynolds's daughter. You know you can't lay a hand on her. He's nearly head of the damn Klan. He's even higher than Daddy. We'll tell him we found her out here and let him deal with her. He'll be happy we reported it," Simpson said flatly as though he were thoroughly unimpressed with the whole situation. But Betty had begun to know his mannerisms enough to see the clench in his jaw, a telltale sign he was nervous.

"Fine, but the other one, there's no reason we shouldn't beat the snot out of her. We can drag her ass back to town and leave her in front of the school as a message to those teachers starting tomorrow. That'll keep them out for sure." Nicky edged closer to Betty and Alma, who were now cowering in fear. Betty looked to Simpson, knowing if he intervened now he'd be paying with his life. If Nicky didn't beat him to death, surely his father would.

"I don't know if we should be doing anything without the Klan knowing about it first. They don't want any heat blowing back on them unless it's something they sanctioned. You heard about all that stuff in Mississippi." Simpson took another few steps forward so he could be at his brother's side.

"Bullshit, if you'd have showed up last night you'd have heard them say it was time to stop this by any means necessary. Burn crosses, toss bricks through windows, make threats, and show force. Maybe Daddy is right about you; maybe you don't have the stomach for it. Maybe you're with them." Nicky turned his attention toward his brother who glared back angrily at him.

"You don't know shit about me," Simpson boomed, shoving Nicky back. Betty felt her heart thud with fear and then realized this must be part of his plan. Simpson would take a licking from his brother and give Betty time to help Alma get away. When Nicky took the bait and grabbed the collar of Simpson's shirt, slamming him against the wall, it cleared the path to the door.

"Run," Betty said, letting go of Alma's hand. She grabbed a piece of wood, leaning against the wall. Standing, she raised it over her head and whacked Nicky in the arm. It made a thwacking noise Betty wasn't prepared for, sounding much worse than she thought it would. "Run," she commanded Alma again, and she finally started moving.

When Nicky realized what was happening he spun, trying to decide if he should chase after Alma or disarm Betty. That wasn't a choice she could allow him to make. She swung again, but he grabbed the wood from her hand, snatching it away. As he looked at the door and made a move to follow Alma, Betty fell to the ground and clutched his leg. He dragged her along for a couple of steps and then raised the wood to strike her.

Glancing up through panicked eyes Betty braced herself for the blow coming her way. But before the contact could be made, Simpson grabbed his brother's arm. "Her daddy will kill you," he reminded his brother.

"Hold her down," he demanded, and Simpson froze at the cold heartless tone of his brother's voice.

"What are you gonna do to her?" he asked, staring down at Betty's dirty clothes and trembling shoulders.

"It won't be nothing compared to what Daddy does to you if I go home and tell him you let a tar-baby get away and then pussied out when it came to making this one pay for hitting me. He'll lynch you himself." Nicky's eyes bore holes through Simpson, and Betty took the opportunity to nod slightly at Simpson. She knew Nicky wouldn't kill her. This was not a life for a life. There was no point in Simpson blowing his cover to save her from getting knocked around a bit, while Simpson would likely get killed if he were exposed.

He leaned down and pried Betty's arm off Nicky and yanked her backward. "What are you gonna do to her?" he asked again, trying to get a read on his brother's maniacal face.

Nicky reached down to his hip and flipped open a pocketknife. The two-inch blade shone in the light that flowed in the cracked walls of the shed. Now Betty worried that she was wrong. Maybe her life wasn't safe just because of her father's position in the Klan.

"Nicky," Simpson whispered as he stared at the blade of the knife. "Think about what you're doing."

"I'm not gonna kill her. I'm just gonna make her sorry for hitting me," Nicky grunted. "Hold her down like you mean it."

Betty stopped fighting against Simpson's grip and held her breath. She had no control over whatever would be done to her. It wouldn't be fair to expect Simpson to stand up for her now. Though her heart cried out for a chance, she let her face go flat.

Nicky ran the small blade across her cheek and the cold steel made Betty close her eyes, not wanting to see her own blood if it were about to spill. But instead of slicing at her skin Nicky took her long braid on the left side of her head and yanked it tight. With significant effort he sawed the blade back and forth until her hair came free and sat in his hand.

She didn't cry. She wanted to, but she couldn't put that burden on Simpson. Nicky slammed her head to the other side and did the same to her second braid.

"You think no one liked you before, wait till they see you now. Wait till they hear what you were doing out here. I wouldn't even bother coming back to town if I were you. Your daddy ain't even gonna want you now." He tossed the braids in Betty's lap and gestured with his head for Simpson to follow him.

Feeling Simpson's arms let her go was the loneliest moment of her young life, and there had been plenty other moments to contend with, so that was saying something. Betty sat motionless until everything was silent. When she was sure Nicky and Simpson were gone, her shaking hands lifted to the sides of her head where her braids used to be. The only thing left were the two tiny elastics that sat snug to her head and a few spikey strands of hair that hadn't cut off clean. She pulled the elastics free and ran her hands across her scalp, realizing her long frizzy brown locks were completely gone. She was grateful there was no mirror here because seeing herself in this moment might break her completely.

The sadness and fear were so powerful tears wouldn't come. Instead, just rapid hyperventilating breaths and hiccups escaped her mouth. She'd never been a vain person. Her looks weren't spectacular nor did she obsess about them, but the idea of being nearly bald, being branded in a way everyone could see, made her shudder with embarrassment. She'd felt like a freak for a long time and been treated like one, but now she looked the part, too. It was more than she could bear.

All of that was crushing her, and she hadn't even let herself worry about what her father would do once he found out the truth. She tossed her braids to the ground and reached for one of the blankets Simpson had brought for them. Curling up on the dirt floor, she lay her cheek against the ground and let it soak in the tears that finally began.

Nicky was right. There was no point in her going home. She might as well stay right where she was and pray that maybe a tornado would scoop her up and take her away. Anywhere she landed would be better than this town.

Chapter Twelve

The noises of the night had started to unhinge Betty as she tightened the blanket around her. Every few minutes she had to convince herself staying out in this shed alone was better than going home. But it was the creaking door that made her most certain she should have left by now.

"Betty," she heard Simpson whisper, and she felt like she'd gone from being the last person on the planet to the luckiest; she finally had a savior.

"I'm here," she replied quietly as she peeked her head out from the blanket and squinted at the bright stream coming from his flashlight.

"I thought you'd still be here. It's not a good idea to stay out here all night by yourself." Simpson edged in closer but didn't meet Betty's eyes. The usual snippy edge to his voice was gone. He sounded very much like a little boy right now.

"They know I'm here, don't they? Your brother would have gone to my house and told them what happened and who I was with. So if they really wanted me home, they'd have come for me." Betty had realized this a couple hours ago and decided it would be the test of her parents love for her. Surely if they'd known she'd been attacked and left alone in the woods, they'd come for her.

"They know," Simpson said, clearly trying to apologize for them. "Your daddy is mad as hell. He's not coming out here. I waited until my folks were sleeping before I snuck out. I can walk you home. I bet your house is quiet by now. You know what Winnie always says: everything looks better in the morning."

"I'm not going back there. Not ever. Not like this." Betty choked on her words as she reached up and touched her mangled hair.

"I'm so sorry," Simpson croaked, dropping his head down and clutching his hands together. "It's my fault. I was a coward. I should have stopped him. I held you down, but what I should have done is turned that knife on him. I'm scum."

"He's scum," Betty shot back as she sat up quickly. "Winnie's right. We can't be soldiers in this; we're kids. It's not up to us what the world wants. We just have to deal with it. I'm not mad at you for what you didn't do. I'd be pissed as hell if you had tried to help me. Who knows what they'd be doing to you right this minute if you had. Winnie's been right about everything. We can't mix. She's got her own war to fight once she starts teaching, and I'm gonna stay clear of it. All of it. If I can't see them anymore then so be it."

"We can find another place. I'll be more careful to make sure no one follows us. It's my fault. I'm sorry. But don't give up." Simpson knelt beside Betty and folded his hands in a begging fashion.

"She likes you, ya know? You're older and nice and cute, and she is starting to get a crush on you," Betty remarked as she stared off at a fluttering piece of dust passing across Simpson's flashlight.

"Alma?" Simpson asked, not seeming to understand the quick change of subject.

"Yep, and if you keep hanging around she's gonna like you more and more. She's a nice girl; she'll get older and be beautiful, and you'll like her back. But you both live in a world where that don't matter a stitch. Don't you think it's better to just let her go now? I didn't think so before today, but then I saw your brother and realized she was the one in the room in real danger. She's the one who's gonna pay if we get caught. I'm already caught. The only thing I can do now is beg my daddy to forgive me, know he won't, and hope he just leaves me alone if I do everything he wants."

"I don't want to go back to the way things were before. I don't want to feel alone while I'm around all those people. You guys are all I got." Simpson's pleading eyes rattled Betty but only for a fleeting moment. As a cool breeze blew through the slats of the shed and across her exposed scalp, she remembered what was true.

"I'll be as bad to be around as she is come tomorrow. You won't dare be seen with me either."

"Then let's go. Let's catch a bus and head north and just say we're brother and sister. We can be orphans. We can make something up. We don't have to stay here." Simpson's words came flying out frantically.

"Yes we do. We don't have to stay here our whole lives but we have to stay here now. The bad you know is better than the bad you don't. At least we know what to expect here. Out there, the world is too big for us."

"I can't let you stay out here tonight. Not by yourself," Simpson said, shaking his head adamantly.

"I'm not leaving." Betty asserted. "Tomorrow I'll go home. I'll take whatever beating I get and then stay out of the way. But tonight this place is gonna be exactly what you said. No one here is gonna tell me anything. I want that for one night."

"Then pass me a blanket. I got six brothers, and my folks don't notice an empty bed." Simpson kicked off his shoes and tucked his sweatshirt behind his head like a pillow.

"You're really gonna stay?" Betty asked, eyeing him skeptically. "Even with someone as ugly as me?" She touched her hair, or the lack thereof, and started to cry again.

"Please don't cry. I can't take the crying. Plus it doesn't look all that bad. It'll grow back. You're not ugly." Simpson locked eyes with Betty, so she knew he meant it.

Chapter Thirteen

"I guess they're gonna let her in today," a kid behind Betty whispered as she settled into her desk at the front of the classroom. It had been twenty-one days of pure hell for Winnie and the four other black teachers who'd been hired to work at Edenville East Middle School. They'd been locked out, chased out, and kicked out of the school every time they tried to go to work. Betty had watched it all from behind the brim of the hat she wore every day now. Pulling it low over her eyes, she managed to pretend she wasn't real most days. The hat was against the dress code, but they'd made an exception considering how awful she looked without it. There were a lot of short styles that people were wearing but her hair was too lopsided and jagged to make any of them work.

"I knew once the National Guard got here there would be no keeping them out," a boy from the back of the class called. "But it don't matter; they can't protect them while they're in here, and they can't make us listen to them."

A couple weeks ago Betty would have stood up in the middle of the class and made a case against that ignorance, but now she just sat silently. She'd convinced her father she was sorry and convinced herself this fight was not hers. Winnie was a grown-up. She could handle herself. Betty had tried to rise above it all, but it didn't matter. They'd won.

Or had they? As Winnie walked across the threshold of the classroom, escorted by a soldier from the National Guard, Betty had a fleeting feeling of victory. But it was short-lived.

The soldiers left the room, and Winnie stood there as though she didn't know what to do with herself, something Betty had never seen from her before. Tipping her hat back slightly, she showed her eyes, and Winnie's glance fell on her. Like electricity they connected, something monumental and undefined happened between them. All Betty could hope was that no one else had seen it.

"I'm Mrs. Winifred Lincoln, I'll be trying to teach you for the rest of the year." She placed her bag down on the desk and eyed the rest of the room.

"Trying?" a little snotty girl who still had her pigtails attached to her head asked.

"Well, whether or not you learn anything will be up to you. It's fine by me if you want to act as though you already know everything. If you leave this room at the end of the year without a stitch more knowledge than when you entered it, you can deal with that. What I won't accept is rudeness toward me or anyone else in this room. You don't need to like me. You don't need to pretend you think I should be here. But at the end of the day I am an adult, an educated teacher who was hired to be here and teach. I deserve a basic level of respect, and you will give that to me." Winnie propped her hands on her hips and eyed them all in a way that finally reminded Betty of the Winnie she knew.

"Or what?" one of the boys asked with a rude snicker. He lounged back in his chair as though he wouldn't entertain the idea of respect for a second.

"Or the exact same thing that would happen to you if I were white. I will stand you up in the corner of this room. I will send you to the principal whether he wants to punish you or not. You will have more work assigned to you than you know what to do with, and if you don't do it, you will fail. Like I said, I couldn't care less one way or the other. But I want to be fair to you and tell you up front how it will work. Any questions?"

The room sat silent, glances passing between all the kids. Two boys, whom Betty knew to be cousins, stood up, grabbed their books, and stormed out of the room. Expletives slipped from their lips as they slammed the door behind them.

"Well that was easier than I thought." Winnie shrugged. "Anyone else want to go? Now's your chance."

Kids shifted in their chairs but didn't make a move to stand. There was grumbling among them but nothing that could be understood.

The rest of the day went on normally. Far more so than Betty would have expected. Though every minute that ticked by didn't find her any more comfortable. The dread and worry that something was about to happen had stayed with her every day since Nicky had cut off her hair.

"Beatrice," Winnie called, shaking her from her trance. "You'll be the first to clean the erasers after school today. Then I'll put a schedule for the rest of the class. Everyone will have a week when they are responsible for it."

Betty wasn't sure if she should say, "Yes, ma'am" or if that would make her seem too kind to someone she was supposed to hate. Instead she just nodded her head and fought the pink that was spreading across her cheeks.

Hours later, the class dismissed. A moaning and complaining huddle of kids dispersed, and soon just Betty and Winnie were sitting in the otherwise empty classroom.

"Betty," Winnie began empathetically, but she was cut off by the wave of her hand.

"You should call me Beatrice. That's my name. That's who I am, and I don't get to change it." She moved toward the front of the classroom and gathered up the erasers.

"I'm so sorry for what happened to you and so grateful for what you did for Alma. She cries every day now. She misses you and Simpson something fierce. I don't know how to help her." Vulnerable wouldn't have been a term Betty used to describe Winnie up until now, but she just looked too damn tired to hold it back.

"She'll get over it. My hair will grow back. We should have listened to you all along. We don't belong mingling like that. It was foolish."

"You weren't just mingling. You're friends. I was wrong to act like you weren't. I can see how broken her heart is, so I know how much she loves you." Winnie reached a hand out to touch Betty's shoulder, but Betty pulled away quickly.

"I'll clap the erasers and bring them back in. I do hope Alma feels better, and I hope you get treated better here. I certainly won't give you any trouble."

"I wouldn't think you would." Winnie sighed, looking like her heart was breaking. "You can come by you know. Alma would want to see you."

"You said I couldn't once school started," Betty shot back, sounding angry when she meant to sound hopeful.

"I know what I said. I don't think I was wrong to say it, but I'm as bad as any of them if I keep you kids apart. I might regret welcoming you back, but I'm already regretting not having you around." Winnie's brows furrowed and her mouth turned down with sadness.

"I promised my daddy I'd be better. I promised him I'd steer clear of—" She thought back to the words he'd used, the anger he'd said them with, and the names he'd called her friends. "What's different anyway? Why invite us back now? We're no safer there. This same thing could have happened at your place," Betty challenged, pulling the hat from her head and exposing the damage Nicky had done.

"The difference is my place," Winnie paused, grabbing Betty's hand and squeezing it tightly. "If they want to do that at my place they'll have to come through me first."

Betty swallowed her emotions and raised her chin as she stacked the last of the erasers. "My mother has a church meeting after school tomorrow. No one would miss me."

"Good, 'cause we miss you," Winnie said with a tiny smile lighting her face.

Chapter Fourteen

Like being in the clutch of a bear, Betty lost her breath in Alma's tight hug. She felt an odd mix of relief and fear.

"I wasn't sure I'd ever see you again, not up close anyway," Alma rejoiced with a buzzing excitement. "I heard what that boy did to you." She tapped at the hat on Betty's head and jumped when she was swatted away.

"Please don't. It looks awful," Betty said solemnly. "I don't want you to see it."

"I don't care what you look like. If I did don't you think I'd have noticed you were white by now," Alma teased.

"I can't stay very long. I'm not supposed to be out of the house at all really. It wasn't until I saw your house that I knew I'd come at all," Betty explained with a sigh.

"We're mighty glad you did," Winnie cut in as she dropped a bagful of vegetables on the counter. "Alma, do me a favor and head down to Cynthia's with these carrots. I promised I'd bring her some."

"But Betty just got here," she protested with a stomp of her foot. With a subtle raise of her eyebrow Winnie quieted her daughter, who snatched the carrots away and headed for the door.

"How are you doing, girl?" Winnie asked, moving toward Betty. "What can I do for you? I'll do anything to take that sadness out of your eyes."

Betty thought on it for a few seconds. Could a slice of Winnie's pecan pie do the trick? Could some of her special feel-better soup make a dent in Betty's heartache? Not likely. "Just," Betty choked out as she dove into Winnie's arms, a place she missed terribly, "please don't turn me out again. No matter what, please don't tell me not to come back. I need to know you're here, and I can be here if I need to be. I just need to know someone loves me, no matter what." Blubbering through sobs, Betty grabbed the soft fabric of Winnie's shirt and held on for dear life.

Winnie struggled to find words, settling for rocking Betty back and forth as she hummed her apologies. "I promise," she whispered into what was left of Betty's hair. "No matter what, you can always come here. You do have people who love you."

Alma thumped her way back through the door and stiffened at the sight of the sheer, unbridled emotion unfurling before her. "What's the matter?" she asked, raking her eyes over the two of them as they sobbed.

"Nothing," Winnie said, straightening Betty up and brushing the wrinkles out of her own apron with a pat of her hands. "We were just coming to an agreement about the future, that's all."

"And what did you agree to?" Alma asked disbelievingly.

"That this door will open anytime she knocks on it. She's not alone. She won't ever be alone," Winnie explained as she stroked Betty's hair.

"It's not safe here, though. I thought," Alma stuttered but was cut short by Winnie's familiar glare.

"It's not safe anywhere." Winnie returned to the job of sorting out vegetables. "Might as well be together."

"What about Simpson?" Alma asked, attempting to look casual.

Betty remembered the last conversation she and Alma had, leading up to the attack in the shed. She'd spent the last few weeks wallowing in her own sadness, so much she'd overlooked how tragic the scenario was for Alma, too. It would be impossible to deal with having a crush on someone you could never be with. Simpson had become a regular around Alma's house, laughing and playing, and then suddenly he was gone. There was nothing fair about the world they lived in, but it seemed doubly cruel when the heart was involved.

"I haven't gotten within a hundred feet of him since that day. I'm a pariah in town now, and I told him he's got enough problems. Hanging around me isn't worth the trouble." Betty flopped into the dining room chair and tossed her tired head back.

"How does he seem? I don't see him in school at all. He's in the other side of the building with the older kids." Winnie looked concerned.

"The last time we talked he wasn't so good. He thought he should have done more to help me that day. He thinks he should have stopped his brother. I told him he shouldn't have, and he isn't a coward. But," Betty paused, looking at her fingers and twisting them nervously, "maybe he should have done something."

"No way," Alma said, jumping to his defense. "That's his brother. If he went back home and told their folks, Simpson would be swinging from a tree by now. He's no coward."

"Easy, child," Winnie commanded, eyeing her daughter skeptically at first and then morphing into a knowing look. "I suppose you care a lot for Simpson, but there's no point wasting the little time we have debating things that don't have answers. Not while there's flour to sift."

"What are we making?" Betty asked, the life bolting back into her body as she stood.

"Bread. We're going to make enough for the week since it seems I'll be working late."

"Why?" Alma asked, still looking cross about Simpson. "They can't keep you there late every day."

"They can if they want to. Someone needs to run the detention class, and I seem like the best person to dump that on."

"But then you won't be able to walk home with Mr. Kape and the other colored teachers," Betty pointed out, realizing how vulnerable that would make Winnie. "Maybe that's why they're doing it. They want to get you alone."

Winnie let out a sad hum. "It breaks my heart knowing you've got to think like that. I know I've had some part in you realizing the world isn't perfect, but I wasn't trying to make you afraid of it." Winnie dusted the counter with flour and reached for the clay canisters that held her other ingredients.

"She's right, Mama. You can't be leaving there late and on your own. People keep saying it's getting worse and worse. They're saying Edenville is at its boiling point." Alma sidled up to her mother and dusted her own hands with flour, getting ready for her job in the recipe.

"You think I'm dumber than a coal bucket? I know better than to be walking back here on my own. Your daddy is changing his schedule at the factory so we can walk home together. Stop worrying your pretty little heads about me, and start measuring that flour so I can teach you the tricks to the perfect yeast dough. It's white vinegar, by the way." With expert precision Winnie brought the ingredients to life in the form of a smooth silky ball. Betty watched in awe as everything else melted away except the earthy scent of rising dough.

Chapter Fifteen

1965 – Edenville

There were a hundred close calls, but there were thousands of cheerful memories made in Winnie's kitchen over the next few years. The world seemed to evolve and then backslide, giving hope and then taking it away, but Edenville found some level ground to stand on. At least for a little while. The schools integrated painfully at first, and then, when people on both sides became exhausted, everything quieted.

"It was forty-six days this time," Alma said, pulling up her calendar. "That's how long you two've been away. I hate that."

"Sorry," Simpson apologized with a shrug. "My daddy has a fire under his ass again about something. Don't know what it is, but something is brewing. We had to lay low for a while."

Simpson had grown into his long legs, and his shoulders had spread as wide as any grown man in town. Betty and Alma teased him often about the shadow of the beard that crept up on his face every few days. The years had changed them all. Alma's missing teeth had all grown into a beautiful smile. And her twiggy body had finally blossomed into the curves she always complained about not having. Betty's hair grew back in with a silky wave and her body caught up with her lanky arms and legs. More shocking than any of nature's changes was the fact they'd all survived and managed to nurture the seed of friendship they'd planted. It was nothing short of miraculous.

"What do ya think it is?" Nate asked as he stepped over the threshold with an armful of logs. Simpson hopped to his feet and insisted on taking the load from him.

Betty grabbed another biscuit from the table and slathered it with jelly. "I heard they're planning attacks on the civil rights leaders. But that was just some kids talking big after school. My mama's kept me on a tight leash. Luckily she was at a planning meeting for the bake sale this afternoon, so I could sneak away. I sure missed these biscuits."

Winnie cleared her throat and shot Betty a look. She could do that now. In this house there was no distinction between Betty, Simpson, and Alma when it came to Winnie's stern looks. They were all subject to a thwack to the back of the head if it came to that.

"What? I missed y'all, too," Betty defended, stuffing another mouthful of biscuit in her mouth. This was sheer heaven. Being away from the love here in this place was torture, but it made the times they were together sweeter. There was nothing like walking into Winnie's kitchen and smelling her food cooking. By this time Betty knew many of her recipes by heart, though she wouldn't dare cook them anywhere else. She'd learned a whole lot more than cooking over the years, though. They all had.

"Well it's good to have you back," Winnie admitted. "I don't like it when we have to go so long without seeing each other. Since Simpson graduated and you moved up, I don't get to see you around school anymore. Anything new to report?"

"I think Simpson has some news." Betty grinned and nudged him in the ribs as he joined them at the table.

"Shut up, Betty, will ya?" Simpson blurted harshly as his face turned pink.

"Oh it must be good, he's blushing," Alma called back as she pointed at his increasingly hot cheeks.

"Margaret Tenner invited him to the Sadie Hawkins dance even though he's already graduated. She's telling everyone she's had a crush on him since last year, and she's sure she can get him to go." Betty spoke animatedly as she watched Simpson's jaw clench tightly.

"A crush since last year," Alma snipped. "That doesn't seem like all that long to have a crush."

Betty bit at her lip, holding back a smile as she realized how long Alma had been daydreaming about Simpson. Almost five years now and somehow they'd all managed not to bring it up and call attention to it, though everyone in the room knew it to be true.

"It's not a big deal. I'm doing it as a favor for my brother, Stan. He's in her grade and he wants to go with her friend. The only way that'll happen is if I go with Margaret. I owe him."

"Why? What do ya owe him?" Betty asked, a scowl taking over her face. Betty lumped all Simpson's brothers in the same heap of social manure no matter how many times he tried to convince her otherwise.

"He's covered for me a bunch. Stan's not like my other brothers. He's helped me stay off my father's radar for a while now. It's just one dance." Simpson picked at the splintered wood of the kitchen table and avoided everyone's stare, especially Alma's. Betty knew full well where Alma stood on the matter of Simpson, but up until this moment she wasn't sure how he felt about her. The color of their skin was still a far bigger gap than their age.

But the look on Simpson's face spoke volumes to how little that mattered.

"Any other news?" Winnie asked, sparing them all by changing the subject. "Are you going to this dance, Betty? They've assigned me to chaperone, so I'd be able to see you all dressed up. I'd love that."

"I wouldn't bother asking anyone. You know no one likes me. I'm still just the idiot girl who doesn't follow the rules of the world." Betty shrugged off the statement, but, truthfully, she wondered if she'd be alone forever. She couldn't think of a single person outside of this house who genuinely cared for her. "My mama sewed a dress for me, but I think even she knows I couldn't get a date."

"Any boy would be lucky to go with you," Nate chimed in with a paternal grunt. "You'll just have to wait until you're older to find a boy who's got some sense in his head."

"Now that I know you'll be chaperoning maybe I'll just go by myself. It's not like people can tease me anymore than they already do. At least I'd get to see you, Winnie." Betty thought through the painful scenario of walking into the gymnasium alone. It wouldn't be comfortable, but nothing outside Winnie's house ever was.

"Do you even know how to dance?" Alma asked Simpson with a face full of doubtful attitude.

Simpson and Betty looked at each other as though they'd completely forgotten that important part of the equation. "I never went to any of the dances before I graduated," Simpson explained. "This girl's not gonna expect me to dance with her, is she?"

"Well what do you think you're going there for?" Winnie asked with a hearty laugh.

"I've got two left feet," Betty said, sticking her saddle shoes out from under the table.

"Looks like you two need a lesson. As much as I'd like to watch you fumbling around on the dance floor looking like a couple of drunken giraffes, I think it's my duty to do something. Alma go fetch the radio from the living room." Winnie gestured for them all to get up as she slid the table against the wall to make more room.

"You're going to teach us to dance?" Simpson asked, looking like he could think of a hundred things he'd rather do.

"Alma is," Winnie announced as her daughter walked back into the kitchen.

"I am?" she shot back incredulously.

"You're a fantastic dancer. Your grandmother taught you, and I know she'd have wanted you to pass that on to someone. Now come on over here, Simpson," Winnie ordered as she shoved the two of them together. "Your hand goes here, and then the other like this," she continued, moving them around like a couple of reluctant store mannequins.

Betty started watching to see if Simpson would be able to learn to dance but it was the way he was looking at Alma that kept her attention. As the music started playing Alma yanked him into motion, leading him around the tiny dirt floor.

"You're too far away from each other I think," Betty interjected and was met with flaring nostrils and dagger eyes from both her friends.

Winnie laughed. "She's right. Move in; I don't think either of you bite."

"Like this?" Simpson asked Alma as he moved in closer and took the lead. "Am I doing it right?" His eyes came up from watching their feet and locked with hers. Alma smiled warmly at him and nodded as the dance became fluid. Betty imagined just like in the movies the world would melt away around them and they'd only see each other. She wished many nights there could be a way for Alma and Simpson to have a real shot together.

"You're not bad," Alma observed after a moment of looking as though words were escaping her. The part Alma couldn't see, the thing that could only be seen from the outside, was the wide-eyed scared look on Simpson's face every time Alma looked away. He wasn't shocked that she danced so beautifully; it looked more like he was stunned by the way it made him feel. There was a glimmer in his eyes, as though he was waking up for the first time in his life and finally seeing vibrant colors.

Betty heard Winnie lean over toward Nate and whisper, "Guess I didn't think this through enough before doing it."

Nate chuckled, "Oh please, I'm betting you thought it out exactly like this. You're the puppetmaster, and we're all handing you our strings."

"I think Margaret will be pleased enough," Alma whispered, looking up at him from under her long lashes.

"Who?" he asked as he stumbled over her foot and nearly pulled them both over. He braced her against his arm. "Sorry."

"I'm fine," she assured him as he held her there a long minute before placing her back on her feet.

"Should we keep going?" Simpson asked, opening his arms for her to step back in.

"Yes," Betty teased, pushing Alma forward again. "I'll put on the next song."

Chapter Sixteen

"Did ya hear?" Simpson asked as he slammed into Betty out in front of the diner. They hardly ever talked to each other in public so Betty knew it must be important. When she shot a confused look back at him, he grabbed her by the wrist and led her quickly off Main Street. Rounding a corner to a path in the woods, he spoke, his hot breath meeting the freezing cold air and making a cloud around them.

"All hell is breaking loose. They just burned down Don and Meryl Chipman's house. The Chipmans were working to get the voting laws changed so Blacks wouldn't have such a hard time registering. Tina Winslow had a cross burned on her lawn last night. Something is going down. I think it's gonna be bad." Simpson's eyes darted over Betty's shoulder to make sure no one was coming.

Betty nodded her agreement. "My daddy is complaining about the vote day and night now. He was talking about how they had been keeping it at bay by making the requirements completely impossible. He said they were having them jump through so many hoops that most black folks were giving up. But now it's the cause everyone's taking up. It's got my daddy up in arms. Probably the rest of the Klan too. What do you think is gonna happen next?"

"No clue. I've got to get to work at the Miller's farm." Simpson pulled his winter hat down tighter on his head. "I'll tell you, though, I'm getting damn tired of doing nothing. I always said I'd wait until I was old enough and then finally speak up. Well I'm a grown man now. It's high time I take up the cause myself."

"You're one guy, Simpson. You can't change anything. You've done a great job staying out of it all. That can be your contribution. Not once have you ever made it worse." Betty hated to hear Simpson talk this way. It was happening more and more lately, and she knew it was only a matter of time before he got himself caught up in things they'd always tried to avoid.

"You know what they say, just because what you can do is small, doesn't mean you shouldn't do it. The only way things are going to change is if guys like me do something. It's the people not being persecuted who need to stand with the people who are," Simpson's voice was growing in strength as he spoke, and Betty gently touched his shoulder, reminding him she didn't need convincing.

"Who have you been listening to, Simpson? I'm not saying I disagree with you, but I've never heard you say these things before. Winnie always tells us to keep our head down and live peacefully." Betty looked over her shoulder to make sure no one was coming.

"There's been a bunch of meetings outside of town. I've been going and listening to what they have to say. I can be an asset to them. I can help. They want to get folks registered to vote, and I agree with them. This isn't just a bunch of people all disorganized. I'm talking about ministers from all different kinds of religions, people of all colors. People are standing up, and I want to be one of them."

"Can I help?" Betty asked. The enthusiasm and conviction in Simpson's voice was catching. She suddenly felt like a hypocrite for doing nothing day after day.

"You shouldn't. Maybe someday when things aren't so violent, but right now it's no place for a girl. Finish school. Just hold the right stuff in your heart like you always have." Simpson patted her shoulder and looked at her empathetically, as though it was quite the curse to be a girl in this world. And he was probably right.

"I know what's right and what's wrong. I know the root of all of this is the idea that some lives are worth less than others. If they could see that wasn't the case, then things would change."

"Just don't go to Alma's. It's not safe right now. Keep your ears open. They might even cancel the dance," Simpson added, looking like he was fighting a smile.

"You look happy about that." Betty grinned.

"I don't want to go to the dance with Margaret. I told you I'm only going so my brother can get the date he wanted. He's the one who got me the job at the Miller's farm, and that's what's kept me from having to get mixed up in too much of my daddy's mess. Mr. Miller knows I want nothing to do with it and, frankly, neither does he. I told him to work me day and night, and he understood what I meant. I've got my brother to thank for that, but it doesn't mean I'm looking forward to dancing with Margaret."

"You'd rather be dancing with Alma?" Betty asked, feeling like she was standing on hot coals while she waited for his much-anticipated reaction.

"Don't be dumb," he scoffed. "Alma is my friend the same way you are."

"Just the same, huh? Cause it seems like maybe you were worried about how she'd feel about you going to this dance. I saw the look on your face when you two were dancing. You know she's liked you since we were kids, right?"

"She's still a kid," Simpson shot back.

"She's fifteen, and you've just barely turned eighteen. That's not that much of a difference. My folks are five years apart. Even Nate is four years older than Winnie," Betty reminded him.

"We can't even be seen in public just being friends in a town like Edenville, you really think we'd just go to a dance together? It's not realistic."

"I didn't ask if you thought going to the dance with her would be a good idea. She doesn't even go to our school. I asked if you wished you were going with her instead."

"You know what Winnie says about wishing. It's as pointless as brushing your teeth while eating cookies. Wishes don't get you anywhere." Simpson folded his arms across his chest as he wielded Winnie's wisdom like a weapon.

"Simpson," Betty crowed, perching her hands on her hips, "just answer me. I swear I won't tell."

Simpson kicked at a pile of leaves that were crunching beneath his feet. "If things were different, which they aren't, I'd like to take Alma to a dance. I bet she'd look real pretty in a nice dress with her hair done up. But don't give me any crap about it. None of it matters anyway."

"It does matter, Simpson. I'm not telling you it will work out or anything. It sounds like everything's going to hell in a handbasket again around here. But don't say it doesn't matter."

"You need to go straight home and stay there tonight. The dance is in two days. You'll see Winnie then. Otherwise, lay low. I think things'll get worse before they get better." Simpson pointed a finger at her, knowing how hard it always was for her to stay away.

"Things always seem to just get worse. I'm still waiting for them to get better." The idea of going back to missing her friends again took any joy Betty was feeling and returned her to reality.

"Don't get all sad. We've done pretty well over the years, and it's been by using our heads. I know you miss them. I do too," Simpson said, trying to comfort her.

"It's different for you," Betty bit back more angrily than she meant to. "People out here still like you. You have other friends. You have a job and a purpose. When I can't be at Winnie's house, it's like I don't exist at all. Look at us; we had to come up in the woods just so you could talk to me. I'm nobody."

"Don't say that, Betty," Simpson demanded. "You don't need a damn person in this town. You've got two more years of school, and then you're free."

"Free to go where? To do what?" she snapped back, feeling suffocated by her lack of options.

"Anywhere to do anything. You're not gonna grow old here in Edenville. Maybe the rest of us will but not you. I know it."

"Alma won't. You know Winnie and Nate have been socking away their money just waiting for a chance to move somewhere else," Betty reminded him with an attitude.

"Oh please. They've been saying that since we met them, and they're still here. If they wanted to go, they'd be gone," Simpson said, shaking his head.

"I think they stayed for us," Betty admitted quietly as she locked eyes with Simpson. "I think they knew we wouldn't make it if they left. They could probably be long gone and happy if it weren't for you and me.

"I never thought of it like that," Simpson said sullenly.

"I think about it all the time. If anything ever happened to them because of me, I don't know what I'd do. I'd never forgive myself." Betty's nervous energy bubbled up, and Simpson clamped his hand on her shoulder.

"Nothing is gonna happen to them. But that's all the more reason to go home right now. Things are unsettled; people will be out looking for fights. We can't give them a reason to pick one with our friends. Winnie will have heard by now too, and she'll have all of them lying as low as possible too. It'll work out."

"You don't know that," Betty reminded him.

"I don't know it, but I believe it." He was starting to sound more and more like Winnie all the time. "Now I'll tell you what won't work out. If you breathe a word to Alma about what I said about the dance, I'll call you a damn liar and make you muck the stalls at the Miller's farm until you stink to high heaven."

"Promise," Betty assured, crossing her heart with her hand. "I already knew anyway. I just wanted to hear it from you."

"Of course you did, you're like a little bratty sister." Simpson tugged on her hair the way he did when they were younger, and she slapped him away as he continued. "And I'm happy to call you family. I'd be dead in the woods it weren't for your pushy, nosy mixing in. You're better than most of my brothers."

"Is Stan really all that different? When Nicky chopped all my hair off I figured the rest of your brothers were just the same. That's why I steer clear of them all."

"Nicky's getting his ass handed to him in boot camp right now. My other three older brothers are gone now, too. My daddy sent one to my uncle in Morrissey to help on his farm, and the other two are moving up in ranks in the Klan in Mississippi. Once that happened the rest of us could take a breather from it all. Stan's a lot like me and my other two smaller brothers will be like him, I hope. The less people on this planet like my daddy the better."

"I hear that," she agreed and waved goodbye.

Betty and Simpson headed out of the woods in separate directions. Walking home, knowing she'd be stuck there for a couple days, was always the hardest.

She crept up the walk to the side of the house to peer in the window. Her father was angrily banging his hand on the table as Mr. Lopis from town matched his anger with a scowl. "This is bullshit," her father exclaimed. "We had solid footing here just a few years ago. The damn news media came in and put a few things on television that made us out to be monsters. Everyone put their tails between their legs and forgot what we are here to do. That's coming to an end. We're getting back to where we used to be."

"It's good to hear you talking like this. People need a fire in their bellies. If more of them start voting, we'll be overrun before you know it. We've got to stop the bleeding by making them bleed." Mr. Lopis leaned back in his chair and puffed out his chest. "What's the plan?"

"Havoc. We need to bring hellfire down every opportunity we get. No plan, no rhyme or reason. Wherever the opportunity arises we push back. There are boys coming in from Mississippi this week. We've got the numbers now." Her father's harsh words made Betty physically ill. She gripped the windowsill and held her breath, trying to figure out what she should do next. Simpson told her to stay home. It was what had worked in the past. But right now she wanted to toss the rules to the side and warn her friends.

Yanking her mittens down tighter to keep out the cold wind, she looked over her shoulder at the woods, leading her back to Alma's house. What was the point of being a daughter of a Klan member if she couldn't take what she learned and help people she loved?

Darting back into the woods, she ran as fast as she could to Alma's house. As the dead leaves crunched below her feet, she imagined she was an Indian princess in woods alive with the spirits of the world. The cold wind was making her feet swift, the tree limbs pointed her way, and the birds sang to cheer her on. The world had become very real around Betty over the years, but she still tried to keep her imagination alive.

However, dreams can be dangerous. They can distract and lull you into a world where you believe you are safer than you are. Luckily Betty woke up from her dream just in time. She heard voices laughing in the distance and dove quickly behind an overturned tree, wedging herself beneath its roots.

The ground was freezing cold, a thick frost crystalizing over it, making an odd type of beautiful. She sat completely still as the voices grew closer. She didn't know who they were or what they were doing out here, but she knew if they saw her this close to the west side of Edenville she'd be in trouble.

"None of them are gonna know what hit them. They'll be coming up with a name for this week in the history books when we're done. Edenville will be famous." The gravelly voice was joined by the laughter of at least two other boys, and Betty realized how outnumbered she was. Her only hope was to stay still and remain unnoticed until they passed by.

"How many crosses have they made?" another boy asked as the voices drew closer.

"At least ten. They've got a list of the biggest troublemakers in town, and they'll be the first to learn a lesson. If they fight back it'll be the last thing they do. They think they've got the law on their side with all this new crap coming down from the government about letting them vote, but the only law around here that matters is the sheriff's department, and they're on our side. There's a war coming, they just don't know it yet."

Betty's churning stomach ached with anxiety. Things hadn't been perfect in Edenville but they'd had a stretch of time where, at least in her life, things had settled down. It was clear that was all about to change.

"You hear that?" one of the boys asked, and they all stopped abruptly. From the sound of it they were no more than ten feet to her left. Closing her eyes she willed her body to cease any type of movement. She even tried to quiet her mind.

"It was just a bird, stupid. Let's go. We need to get back and help out with the gasoline. Those crosses aren't going to burn themselves."

When their voices trailed far enough away, Betty uncurled her aching legs and began to cry. She rested her cheek on the thick root of the overturned tree when suddenly something caught her eyes. Bursting up through the frost-covered ground were the most vibrant magenta flowers she'd ever seen. The trees had all lost their leaves; the bushes were all void of color. Nothing but cold air existed out here now except this one bunch of flowers. Like a flood of memory sweeping her away, Nate's words filled her head. She leaned down and plucked one of the flowers from the ground and examined it. Though it was covered in sparkling ice crystals it still thrived vibrantly, defying all Betty knew about nature.

She bolted toward Alma's house with the flower in hand. It was later than she'd normally be arriving, but she had too much to report to turn back now.

"Winnie," she whispered as she let herself in the side door. "I've got something to show you."

"What are you doing here so late? We were just sitting down to dinner." Winnie said, pointing to the table covered with food.

"I'm sorry. I just heard my daddy talking, and I had to come tell you what was happening so you could stay safe. It's gonna be bad." Betty tried to catch her breath as she stepped in front of the kitchen fire to warm herself.

"What's that you're holding?" Nate asked, peeking out the window at the same time making sure no one was around.

"I was sitting out in the woods hiding from some boys who were passing through. They were talking about the war that's coming 'round here and all the things they had planned."

"Did they see you?" Alma asked, looking scared that Betty may have had another run-in with trouble on her way back there.

"They didn't. But as I sat crouched under this fallen tree I saw this." Betty stretched the flower out in front of her for them all to see. The light streaming in through the window caught the magenta petals and seemed to sparkle. "Nate, a long time ago when Simpson and I first started coming here I heard you tell Winnie that trying to help us would just break her heart. That loving kids like us in a world like ours was like trying to grow flowers in the snow. And you were right." Betty stepped closer to them and handed the flower to Winnie. "For a flower to grow in the winter it takes something special. A fortitude that most flowers don't have. But the ones that do have what it takes are the most beautiful of all. It's not likely for flowers to grow in the snow, but it's not impossible."

Winnie took the flower and brought it to her nose, breathing in the scent. "That's very poetic," she said through a quivering voice.

"I hope you know I've always wanted you and Simpson here," Nate said, standing and putting an arm around his wife. "It's never been a matter of me wanting you to leave."

"I know that," Betty said earnestly. "I don't know if I'll ever be able to thank you both for what you've done for me. I didn't bring that, implying any of it's been easy. I don't know another couple of souls in the world who'd have let us keep coming back here. And I know we wouldn't have grown into anything without you."

"You're about to get the waterworks going here," Winnie chuckled as she used the corner of her apron to wipe her eyes.

"What's the news you came to tell us?" Nate asked, looking concerned as he squeezed Winnie's waist a little tighter. "Do they have some plan?"

"That's the problem, I don't think they have anything specific. If they did you could steer clear. The only rule they're going by is the idea of starting a war. It could be anywhere. It could be anyone." Betty slipped her hat off her head and tucked it under her arm. "So I guess the question is, what's our plan?"

Chapter Seventeen

"Why is it every time I want my hair to curl it goes straight, and every time I try to make it straight it curls?" Betty asked her mother as she stepped out of the bathroom wearing her dress. She finally felt like she could fill something out in a way that made it clear she was a woman.

The ivy green sheath hugged Betty's curves tighter than any clothes she'd ever worn. The chocolate brown belt was an afterthought her mother had slipped on her. Bell sleeves with lace trim was the latest fashion, and Betty was shocked her conservative mother had allowed it in her design. She certainly didn't follow the same lead when it came to the length of the dress. Most girls these days were showing much more than knee, but Betty wouldn't be tonight.

"I bought you some flowers," her mother said with a smile as she pinned a small corsage to Betty's dress. Stepping back, her mother took stock of Betty with a sparkle in her eye. "You look very pretty. I think your hair is perfect."

It was so out of character for her mother to deliver a compliment that Betty couldn't hide the surprise she was feeling. "Thank you for making this dress, Mama. Is everything all right?"

"I know you've been spending all your time out on the west side with that black teacher and her family," she said, looking Betty square in the eye.

"I-I . . . um," Betty stuttered, but her mother quieted her instantly with a wave of her hand.

"Don't lie. I'm not angry."

"You're not? But Daddy—"

"Your daddy isn't ever gonna know. He can't."

"But how did you know? Why aren't you upset?" Betty had feared this moment for years but never expected it would go this way.

"I've known for a little while now. I haven't said anything to anyone, especially your daddy. Since I found out, I've been doing a lot of thinking. The world's a complicated place, and everyone deserves somewhere to go where they can feel like themselves. After I thought about it for a while, it made me sad you had to go looking for that somewhere else. I'm sorry you don't feel like this house is a place for you."

"It's not that, Mama," Betty said, trying to dull the hurt her mother must be feeling. "We just see things differently that's all. You and Daddy—"

"Please don't lump me in with him. I've done my share of bad things in my life but, I can tell you, the last few years have opened my eyes to plenty. Not everything is the way your Daddy says it is." She wiped away a stray tear. Betty knew exactly how hard it was for her mother to admit that. She'd spent years idolizing and praising her husband. To see him as anything less than a god among men must have been an earth-shattering revelation for her. "But I suppose you figured that out long before I did."

"What are you saying, Mama? You don't agree with the Klan? You don't agree with Daddy?" Betty felt a small glimmer of hope that maybe she and her mother could be on the same side of something for once.

"It doesn't matter what I think. My time to speak up has passed by already. I'm your father's wife. I've got my place in all this, and there isn't much I can do. But you, I can see you're trying to be different. Different is the hardest thing to be sometimes." She leaned in and adjusted the flowers she'd pinned to Betty's dress. "You deserve better than what you've gotten so far. I can't do much, but I can show you in little ways that I see you. I see what you're doing."

It felt as though she were falling just short of saying she was proud, but to Betty it was close enough. The last few years her mother had grown quieter when it came to her father's rants. Rather than chiming in, she tended to busy herself with other things. Until now Betty hadn't tuned in to the change.

"What do I do, Mama?" Betty asked, crumpling into her mother's arms. It was a question she'd been dying to ask for so long. No matter how their relationship had unfolded over those years, there was never a moment Betty hadn't hoped she and her mother could find something to bring them together and somehow fix all of this for her with some advice and a hug.

"Beatrice, just keep being yourself. It's brave. I envy that about you. Go tonight; have fun. Stay out of your daddy's way, and wait for things to get better."

"What if they don't? It sounds like something is about to happen in Edenville. Everyone is talking about it." Betty's nerves boiled back to the surface as she realized her mother couldn't actually fix anything.

"It might not be today, sweetheart, but right will win out. It always does."

"What changed your mind, Mama? I have to know." Betty prayed for something profound, some moment that would make all the pieces of her understanding make sense.

"There was no one thing, just lots of small ones. I started catching more of the news. I started really

137

listening in church. I started listening to you. I'm not saying I want to go pick up a sign and join the protest. It's not all cut and dry like that. But your secret is safe with me." She looked down at her wrist and checked her watch. "You look absolutely stunning. Go make the boys regret not being nicer to you."

Betty slipped on the low-heeled shoes her mother had let her borrow and pulled on her pretty coat. As she made her way toward the school she couldn't help but smile so wide her cheeks ached. Nothing was all that different yet somehow everything was.

Chapter Eighteen

"Betty?" Simpson asked with wide eyes as she stepped through the double doors of the school gymnasium. "You look . . . I mean you don't even look like you."

"Um, thanks, I guess," Betty scoffed as she adjusted one of the pins holding her hair in place.

"I just mean I've never seen you in a dress like that before or with makeup. You look really pretty." Simpson tried to correct himself.

"Pretty and not like myself at all. You might want to work on those compliments. Not that it matters anyway. I'll be the only one here without a date. All dressed up for no reason."

Simpson broke into a smile that told Betty he knew something she didn't, and that was always scary. "You're not exactly the only person here without a date. Stan's date stood him up. She got the chicken pox or something. Stan is here alone, too."

"Don't you dare," Betty commanded, pointing a finger in his face.

Before Betty could grab him, Simpson was darting off. A few seconds later he returned with his younger brother, moping behind him.

"This is Stan," Simpson said with a grin. "You guys must see each other around school and stuff; you're only a grade apart. I figure since I'm stuck with Margaret all night and neither of you have a date you might as well keep each other company." The smirk on Simpson's face was mischievous but sweet.

Trying to dodge any protest, Simpson disappeared into the crowd gathering by the punch bowl.

"I'm sorry," Betty said, trying to find something in the room worth staring at other than Stan. Simpson had been right; she'd seen him around school plenty and while he didn't hassle her, he didn't pay any attention to her either.

"What are you sorry for?" Stan asked, furrowing his brows and running his hand through his reddish brown hair, a sharp contrast to Simpson's dark shaggy mop. Otherwise they shared a lot of features. The almond-shaped eyes that wrinkled at the edges when they smiled and the cavernous dimples at the side of their cheeks were nearly identical.

"I'm sorry Simpson stuck you with me. It won't hurt my feelings if you go over with your friends instead." Betty continued to seem distracted, but really she was avoiding Stan's blue eyes.

"Why would I do that when there is a beautiful girl like you right here? I should be the one apologizing." The compliment rolled off his tongue so smoothly Betty nearly missed it. Forget being called beautiful, just the fact that someone was being nice to her was new.

"I don't understand," she shot back, finally turning to face him head-on. "If you care anything about your reputation, you won't be seen over here with me."

"My reputation was wrecked plenty by most of my brothers who came before me. I know what Nicky did to your hair a couple years back. I'm not like that, but I can see why you wouldn't want spend time with his kin. I wouldn't blame you." Stan ran his hand over his short red hair again.

"My hair grew back." Betty shrugged, trying to make Stan feel less uncomfortable with the gene pool he was forced to share. She'd seen what it had done to Simpson over the years, so she knew Stan likely dealt with much of the same guilt by association.

"It grew back beautifully. I really like the way you have it up like that."

"Thanks," Betty murmured with a blush as she peeked over Stan's shoulder. "It looks like Margaret has her hooks in Simpson now."

"That's who we should feel bad for. I'd hate to be stuck with Moody Margaret for a night. I'm going to owe him big." Stan laughed.

"He said he owes you pretty big for helping him get the job on the farm. It keeps him really busy," Betty said, forgetting for a moment Stan wouldn't know how friendly she and Simpson were.

"I learned pretty early on if I didn't want to be like my daddy and my brothers, then I'd have to be busy. Simpson and I make money and give it to our daddy. It's like paying him to leave us alone. I've still had to do plenty of stuff I'm not proud of and listen to things I don't agree with, but for the most part my hands are clean." Stan gestured for Betty to follow him to a couple chairs against the wall.

"You ever think about doing more? Trying to change things for real?" Betty smoothed her dress flat as she sat and crossed her legs at the ankles. She wondered if Simpson's recent activist chatter was rubbing off on his brother or if she was one of the only people he told.

"With a family like mine that'd be a death sentence. Me being dead doesn't really help anyone. That's what I figure anyway. I just try to do no harm, even if I can't fix things."

"But you believe in equality?" Betty pressed.

"You really are the way people talk about you, aren't you? You want to make waves?" Stan flashed his crystal eyes as he looked her up and down trying to get a read.

"I don't want to make waves, I want the sea to be calm. I want everyone to be able to swim." Betty straightened her back in the chair as though she were readying for a challenge. She didn't speak out often these days; there wasn't a point, but she felt like he had the wrong idea about her.

"Wow," Stan dropped his eyes from her and bit at his thumbnail, "I've never met anyone like you."

"That's because it's hard being someone like me. It's lonely." She hadn't meant to sound so depressing, but sometimes that's just what the truth was.

"I'll be your friend." Stan shrugged, as though it were no big deal. But Betty knew he wasn't thinking it through.

"But everyone would—" Betty began to explain, but Stan cut her off by hopping to his feet.

"Let's dance. I was practicing for that other girl I was supposed to come here with. Now I'm glad she got the chicken pox." Reaching out his hand like a fairy-tale prince he patiently waited while Betty scanned his expression for sarcasm or a prank. When she was satisfied he meant what he was saying, she placed her hand in his, and they stepped out onto the dance floor.

When his hand touched her waist she felt her heart leap into her throat. They began to move slowly in a circle, nothing fancy, as he led her through the dance.

"I like this song," Betty whispered as she swallowed back her nerves.

Stan pulled her in another inch as he leaned his chin against her temple. "Is there music playing?" he asked gently. "I can't hear anything or see anything but you."

"That's good because I'm sure by now everyone is staring. I'm sure your friends are plotting a way to embarrass us by now."

"I can't see anything but you," Stan repeated and Betty shook her head slightly in agreement. Pulling her in the rest of the way Stan's hand slipped to her back and she rested her head on his shoulder.

If only it could be like this forever.

Chapter Nineteen

It had all happened so fast it wasn't until the second song Stan and Betty had danced to that she realized she'd forgotten to look for Winnie.

"Have you seen any of the chaperones?" Betty asked as the music changed to a faster tune, and they broke away from each other.

"A few, but are you looking to find them or avoid them? I'm very interested in your answer." Stan raised a brow at her, and she blushed at his teasing.

"I, um, one of the chaperones was a teacher of mine. I just wanted to say hello. Oh, there she is," Betty said, seeing Winnie's bright smile from across the room. "Would you excuse me for a minute?"

"Why don't I go with you?" Stan offered, resting his hand on the small of her back.

"I'd like that," Betty cooed as she crossed the room, trying to ignore all the eyes on them. "Hello," she said to Winnie as she busied herself getting a glass of punch.

"Having fun?" Winnie asked, brushing some lint off her pastel pink church dress.

"More than I thought I would," Betty answered with a giggle as she nodded her head toward Stan. "This is Simpson's brother, Stan."

"Nice to meet you," Stan said with a nod of his head. "You both know my brother?"

"Well we, um . . ." Betty stuttered. As Winnie opened her mouth, presumably to save the day, a loud thundering boom shook them all.

"What was that?" Betty asked, clutching Stan's arm.

"I don't know but it sounded close by. We should get out of here, I think." Stan laced his fingers with Betty's and tried to lead her away.

"What about Simpson? Winnie have you seen him?" Betty searched the room for her friend, but as people began to panic she lost her bearings.

"He can take care of himself. He'll be fine. That sounded like an explosion. Look, there's some smoke out there." Stan pointed out the front window of the gymnasium. "Something's going down. We should go."

"He's right," Winnie agreed, patting Betty's shoulder. "Go straight home. I'll find out what's going on, and if I see Simpson, I'll send him home too. Just go on."

"I don't think you should," Betty cried out over the raising voices of the nervous kids around her. "I think it might be something bad. You should go home too."

"I can't. It's my job to be here and keep everyone safe. It'll be fine. Just head home." Winnie disappeared into the crowd and headed for the door to investigate.

"Betty," Simpson called, slamming into both of them. "There you are. Stan take her straight home for me. Someone set Mr. Kape's car on fire, and it blew up. There's a crowd out there, and they're pissed off."

"White hoods?" Stan asked, grabbing Simpson's shoulder before he could leave again.

"Loads of 'em."

"Winnie's out there. We can't leave her. We have to do something," Betty cried, imploring Simpson's help.

"I will," Simpson assured her as he pushed his way back through the crowd.

"I'm not leaving until I know they are both safe. They're my friends." Betty pulled herself free of Stan and started following Simpson outside.

"You're where he disappears to? It's her too, that teacher. That's where he spends his time when I can't find him?" Stan asked, racing to keep up with her.

"Yes," Betty admitted. "They're out for blood. Winnie doesn't deserve that. We have to help."

"Betty, wait," Stan said, snatching her arm up again. "Both our daddies are out there right now. Every angry white guy in town is probably gathering. I know you don't want anything to happen, but there's nothing we can do. Not now."

"I'm tired of hearing that. I've been biting my tongue for the last five years. I'm not letting anyone touch her." Betty yanked free again and pushed her way outside.

Standing in a perfect square around a burning cross were about thirty people in white hoods. They ranged in size from small boys to grown men, all holding flaming torches over their heads. As more kids spilled out of the school, the rumbling of their voices fell silent. Everyone stared at the Klan members just waiting for something to happen. And then it did.

One of the men broke ranks and stepped toward the crowd. Mr. Kape, whose car had just exploded, stood at the head of the crowd of kids looking as though he was trying to protect them. But Betty knew these white kids weren't likely in danger; it was the teacher who should be hiding behind them.

"We've been quiet too long," the man behind the white hood said loudly, projecting his voice for all to hear. "We've allowed our schools to be taken over. We've allowed our jobs to be stolen. Our bloodline is being muddied, and we're putting an end to it. We'll be quiet no more." The man raised his torch high, and the crowd of other men behind him all cheered so loud that Betty jumped, clutching Stan's arm again. "What are they gonna do?" she whispered, but Stan didn't answer. Either he didn't know or he didn't have the courage to say.

Mr. Kape raised his hands as if to show he wasn't intending to fight. "There are kids here. Your kids. They don't need to see this. Send them all home."

"You don't tell us what to do. You see, that's the problem. You think you get the run of the place now. We give you a little, and you want to take the whole damn thing." The hooded man swiped his torch in Mr. Kape's direction, sending him jumping backward, stretching his arms out to protect the children behind him.

"Go on home kids, all y'all go home," Winnie commanded, shooing children who were frozen like statues away. Many did leave. They ran toward the road. But some stayed. Betty knew some wanted to see the show. Their fathers were standing in a square wearing robes, and they didn't want to miss what would happen next.

"Shut up," the hooded man shouted at Winnie as he raised his hand and slapped her across the face. Winnie stumbled backward but stayed on her feet.

"No," shouted Betty but Stan quickly grabbed her waist to keep her from running forward.

"Quiet Betty. Please don't say anything. If you're really her friend, and she's yours, then she'd want you to stay safe," Stan begged.

Mr. Kape jumped to Winnie's side and steadied her. "I'm fine," she announced as she straightened herself up. "What do y'all want? What are you intending to do here?" she asked, looking more confident than she should.

"We've made you feel far too welcome in this school over the years. Tonight, we're gonna make sure you never come back," a second man in a hood said as he stepped forward, a torch in one hand and a brick in the other.

"We should go back inside, find the phone, and call the police," Betty said, frantically trying to catch her breath.

"The police are here, Betty. They're just in different uniforms tonight," Stan sputtered sadly.

"This old truck too," one young Klan member yelled as he pointed at the parked vehicle belonging to one of the other colored teachers. With that some men charged forward and smashed the glass. Others dumped gasoline inside then tossed their torches.

"Maybe that's it. Maybe they'll just burn stuff tonight." Betty hoped as she leaned in closer to Stan. "Maybe that's it."

"Round them all up. You know which ones they are. You know how they sympathize and try to help them. Round them up and bring them here," the first man in the hood demanded, sending the rest of the men into motion.

"They won't bother you," Stan assured her as he pulled her backward. "Your daddy and my daddy are here. They'll leave us alone."

Betty wanted to shout that she didn't care. She wanted to be defiant and brave, but all she could feel was relief that Stan was probably right. She watched Winnie retreat as the men moved toward her, torches in hand.

"Stop," she heard Simpson shout as he stood between Winnie and the mob. "Leave her alone. You're not going to beat a woman are you? Right out here in front of all these kids?"

"Get out of the way, boy. Man, woman, or child—we're done discriminating. If they try to infiltrate our way of life we will knock them back to theirs. Get the ropes boys, we're gonna drag them back to their side of town."

"Run, Winnie," Simpson said flatly. "Get home. Warn everyone." Simpson grabbed the knife he normally carried on his belt for his work on the farm and let the blade catch the light of the torches. The men stopped in their tracks for a moment. Betty swallowed hard and moved forward through the small remaining crowd until she reached Winnie.

"Go," she urged her friend. "They'll kill you. If you don't warn everyone then who will? You've got to think of Alma. Go."

Winnie's eyes welled with tears as she looked helplessly at Betty. Turning on her heel, she kicked off her shoes and headed for the woods. When three men lunged at Simpson he backed them off with a swipe of his knife. But two others got past and tried to follow Winnie. Betty held her breath and dove in front of them, her body hitting the ground with a thud and tripping them both.

The second burning vehicle popped, hissed, and then exploded. It rattled the crowd for a moment and gave Winnie the jump she needed to get away. But before Betty could get back to her feet on her own she was being pulled up by many hands.

"Daddy please, help me, Daddy," she called into the sea of white hoods. She knew her father was there. She knew he could hear her pleas. Her limbs were being yanked in every direction as she tried to dig in her heels.

They threw her down into the circle of people who'd been rounded up.

"Go on," she heard her father say as he lifted her up and pushed her out of the group. "Go on home."

She'd been spared by her father but only reluctantly so. She wanted to search the group for Simpson to plead for him to be spared as well but the chaos raged on. The colored teachers, some white folks, and a few colored who Betty didn't recognize, all huddled together with shocked and horrified eyes as the Klan closed in on them like a predator after its cornered prey.

Stumbling her way free as her father turned his back on her and faced the job he had at hand, Betty felt her body begin to take over. Her feet became swift, and when fight or flight was the only option, she flew.

"Betty," she heard Stan call as he caught up to her. "Are you all right? Are you hurt?"

"I—I, what do we?" she couldn't form a complete thought as Stan pulled her into the darkness of the woods.

"It's okay, they can't get you out here," he assured her as they ducked behind a large formation of rocks. "We'll be all right."

Betty believed him for a moment until the eerie silence broke wide open with screams. Shrill high screams of terrified women mixed together with the painful howls of men. Betty covered her ears, but it wasn't enough to block it out. "Simpson," she mouthed to Stan through a sob. "Simpson."

Chapter Twenty

Stan tried a dozen times to get Betty to leave the woods after the world fell mostly silent again. "I can't leave you out here, and I can't take you back there," he pleaded. "I have to go look for my brother, but I can't until I know you're safe."

"He's my friend," Betty said emphatically. "He's my best friend. Just because the world didn't know, doesn't mean it isn't true. I'll go with you."

"It's probably not safe," Stan said, grabbing a large rock from the ground and holding it like a weapon.

"It's the school I've been going to since I was five. It's not safe. That tells me nowhere is."

They crept out of the woods, Stan leading the way. The smell of burning rubber singed her nose. Smoke was the first thing she could see as they approached the school again. It billowed up from the carcasses of the cars that had been burned to next to nothing.

Stan stepped slowly and silently, making sure not to snap a twig under his feet. Betty had expected the place to be deserted, judging by the quiet, but she was wrong. The crowd had been replaced by a new one. Instead of the riled up and hooded group, there was a somber and stunned growing group of people who all looked like they'd forgotten how to speak. White and colored folks alike—mostly women—covered their mouths and noses, closed their eyes, and turned their heads. Then the silence was shattered again.

"No!" a young black woman hollered as she rounded the corner of a parked vehicle and fell to her knees. "They've killed them. They've killed them all," she cried.

The crowd rushed over and more shrieks rang out. People began running for water to toss over the smoldering bodies that lay in a pile on the ground like discarded trash.

"Simpson?" Betty asked, hiding her eyes and waiting to hear if Stan could tell her more.

"Back up everyone, back up right now," a sheriff said as he shined his light in their faces. "This is a crime scene, and you're stepping all over it."

"My brother," Stan called out. "Is my brother there?"

"They're too badly burned to sort them out here," the officer replied with genuine sorrow in his eyes. "We'll get the names of anyone missing and piece it together."

"That's my husband," one woman cried out. "I can see his wedding ring on his hand."

Others stepped forward and elbowed their way past the officer. "That's my wife's necklace; she's still wearing it," a man bellowed before falling down to his knees.

"Stan, wait," Betty begged, latching on to him before he could break away.

"I've got to know. I have to know if he's there." She felt him break free from her grip, but she stayed put, not feeling strong enough to see something so horrible. "That's a piece of my brother's shirt and his knife there." Stan backed up until he bumped into Betty and together they just kept moving away.

"Stan," a woman's voice bellowed sternly from behind them. "What are you doing with her?"

"Mama," Stan moaned in a pained voice. "It's Simpson. They've killed him. They burned him." He ran his hands over his head again and again like an involuntary tick.

"He pulled a knife. He turned his back on this family," the puckered-face woman in the fur trimmed coat said through angry lips. "He's not my son. If you know what's good for you, come on home now. Be with your father. Show your support." She gestured for Stan to follow her, but he didn't move.

"I'm not coming home right now," Stan replied firmly, looking at his mother as though she'd been possessed by some evil spirit. "Your son, my brother, is dead. You don't have to believe in what he did to mourn him. We have to take him home not just leave him here like it never happened. I want to talk to the police and tell them what I saw."

"You can do what you want. But we won't be burying him. We won't be talking to the police. He made his choices, and he suffered the consequences of his foolishness. They can do with his body what they want." Though her face was cold and unemotional there was something in her eyes that couldn't be snuffed out. It's not possible to completely extinguish a mother's love, no matter what the circumstances. It's an eternal flame.

As Stan made a move forward toward his mother, Betty caught his hand. She wasn't sure if he was stepping in that direction to leave with her or to give the tongue-lashing she deserved, but either way Betty felt compelled to stop him. And he let her. When the moment between them hung thick and silent, his mother finally turned away.

"I need to go find Winnie," Betty announced, a chill running through her body for the first time. She'd likely been cold since the moment she stepped outside hours ago, but her adrenaline had kept her from feeling it. Now it was all she could feel. Stan slipped his sweater off and handed it to her. Though it left him in just a white undershirt, he ignored her protest and insisted she put it on.

"We're not going to Winnie's. We have a responsibility to talk to the police and tell them everything we saw and who we knew under those hoods. Then I'm taking you somewhere safe. My brother asked me to do one thing. He wanted you out of here, and I should have done that. If he cared about you that much, then I owe it to him to make sure you're all right," Stan explained as she stared over his shoulder at the police who had begun to gather. Some had likely shed their white hoods and returned. Others who genuinely cared about this town were probably as sick to their stomach as he and Betty were.

"You already have. You helped me plenty tonight. I'm so sorry about your brother. I'm so sorry that your mother . . ." Betty trailed off not sure there was a word in the English language for what his mother had just done. "I'm just so sorry," she repeated feeling as if she were walking through a dream world. Her heart was shattered, but she couldn't muster tears yet. It was like someone had paused her senses, knowing if she were able to feel them now, she wouldn't survive.

Another officer came up and pointed his flashlight in their faces. "You kids were here when it happened?" he asked with a toothpick between his lips.

"Were you?" Stan asked, eyeing him angrily.

"I wasn't. I wouldn't have been. I can assure you of that. Listen, those folks over there told me your brother is one of the dead."

"Murdered," Stan corrected as he clenched his hands into tight fists.

"You're right. I'm sorry. I want you to know the FBI has been called in already. This isn't gonna go unnoticed by the world. I promise." The officer pulled a notebook from his pocket and a pen from over his ear. "Can I get your brother's information so I can contact your parents?"

"They already know," Stan said, looking down at Betty as though he was giving her a chance to stop him. When she stayed silent he continued, "My mother was just here letting me know my brother was trying to protect an unarmed defenseless black woman from a mob, and he's dishonored our family. She doesn't want his body. She doesn't want to seek any kind of retribution. As far as she's concerned, justice has been served. My daddy will already know what happened because he was here."

"Was he killed too?" the officer asked, looking around as if he'd missed something important.

"No, I'm sure he's fine. Maybe a bit banged up from beating people to death but otherwise probably feeling pretty great tonight." Stan met the officer's confused gaze and his fierce stare made it clear he was telling the truth.

"You need to be seen by the doctor. Both of you. Young lady, you've got some good scrapes on your face that need cleaned up. Has anyone called your folks?"

"Beatrice?" her mother's voice rang out frantically. "Beatrice are you here?"

"That's my mother," Betty said, pointing to a woman with curlers in her hair and a robe wrapped tight around her.

"She looks worried sick," the officer said with a half-smile, as though it was good news to have a mother who didn't want you dead.

155

"Oh Beatrice, thank heaven you're all right. Come on, we need to get you home." Her mother grabbed her two hands and squeezed them tightly.

"I need to go check on my friend. I don't know if she's hurt." Betty looked at Stan for backup, but he didn't provide it.

"She lives on the west side." Stan explained, looking knowingly at the police officer.

"It's not safe there right now. There are officers trying to help but you couldn't go there now. If you give me her name I can check on her and call your house to let you know how she is."

"You best not," Betty's mother cut in. "My husband wouldn't want that. We'll work it out on our own. All I care about right now is my daughter, and she's alive."

"There are people over there who aren't." Betty turned toward the area where Simpson had died, where she could have easily died tonight, and implored her mother to look as well. "They pulled people from the crowd and set cars on fire. They murdered them. They pulled me over there too. If Daddy hadn't yanked me out of there, I'd be dead."

"Your father was here too?" the officer asked, taking a renewed interest in the details now that he knew Betty was in the mix first hand.

"We're leaving. She's not gonna say anything else tonight," her mother insisted as she tried to lead Betty away.

"I think these two are probably in shock. He's just lost his brother, and she saw it all. They should get checked out by the doctor before they go anywhere." The officer pointed over to the medics who'd gathered at the entryway of the school. "And son, I'm truly sorry about your brother. Did he have a date here with him tonight, a girlfriend we should talk to?"

"Oh no," Betty said, clutching her heart. "How am I going to tell Alma? How am I going to tell her he's dead?" And just like that the mechanism that had held her raw emotions at bay came free, and the solid ground below her feet crumbled. "He's dead," she cried. "How am I going to tell her?" The words kept coming, the same question over and over again. People closed in around her, but she couldn't figure out exactly who they were. They sat her gingerly on the ground and talked in her ear, but she couldn't hear them. Simpson was dead. The last five years of her life that were tethered to his friendship seemed to float away. She didn't want to live in a world where this could happen. She didn't want to breathe the same breath as people who could murder her friend. She didn't want to see the look on Alma's face when she heard the truth.

She closed her eyes and wished she never had to open them again.

Chapter Twenty-One

Winnie once said grief was the last connection you have to someone. The deeper the love shared the more cavernous the grief. The days after Simpson's death were a testimony to Betty's love for him. She fell into an impossibly deep darkness. It was like having an abundance of love with nowhere to put it anymore.

True to her word, Simpson's mother had ensured there had been no funeral. The promise of the FBI had been a hollow one. A rumor that failed to come true. In fact nothing had changed in the immediate wake of all the murders. The media arrived and left, moving on to something more pressing somewhere else. Their tragedy was plowed under by another. It seemed unimaginable that any catastrophe could overshadow what happened in Edenville, but there were things happening all over the country that were as pressing but fresher. In Betty's heart this was a travesty of epic proportions, and it saddened her to imagine it was just a drop in the ocean of heartbreak across the country.

"You'll need to eat something eventually," Betty's mother whispered. Sweeping a warm hand against Betty's cool forehead she brushed her bangs from her eyes. "If you don't I'll have to fetch the doctor again. They may put you in the hospital. We don't want that. Your daddy wants you back on your feet before people start talking. Just have a little soup."

Betty closed her eyes and rolled to her side, turning her back on her mother. She hadn't started out angry, but that's exactly where she found herself now. Raging inside, she couldn't fight the distain she felt for her father's violence and her mother's complacency. For the way all of Edenville had failed their children.

"I'm not bluffing you," her mother reiterated. "I'm going to fetch the doctor if you haven't eaten that soup by the next time I come up. You don't want me to send your daddy up." Her mother's show of warmth the other day was quick to evaporate. That's what happens when something doesn't run deep; it's swift to disappear under the heat of reality.

A knock at the front door caused Betty to pull her blanket up to her chin, closing it like a cocoon around her.

"I'll go see who it is," her mother groaned as she slipped out of Betty's bedroom door. "Eat something."

A few minutes later she heard a light tap that let her know whoever had knocked on the front door was there to see her.

"Betty?" Stan asked gingerly. "Your mama said you weren't really up for company, but I have something to tell you."

"What is it?" Betty asked, not bothering to turn over. "What could you possibly tell me that would make me feel any better?"

"I never said it would make you feel better. I just said I had to tell you something. I can't even make myself feel better." Stan stepped in and leaned against her wall.

At the thought of his pain, in what they both must be feeling, she decided to roll over. The thought that misery loved company was a hollow one. Stan's eyes, red from crying, did not make Betty feel better. "I'm sorry. I just can't believe he's gone. I have so much left to tell him," she croaked.

"Me too," Stan admitted as he rubbed at the muscle in his neck. "I just keep thinking I'll wake up, and he'll be back on the top bunk in our room. He was the best of my brothers and he's gone. I think he could have really done something in this world, but now we'll never know."

"I'll always wonder what he would have grown up to be," Betty sighed as she pulled herself up to a sitting position. Her entire body ached with grief, and her chest felt like it might cave in.

"I've got to tell you about your friend Winnie," Stan said biting nervously at the inside of his cheek.

"I already know she got home safe. Simpson saved her life. I got word yesterday. I haven't gone down there yet because I can't bear to face them." Betty wiped at the corners of her stinging eyes with the rough edge of her blanket. "Plus my daddy, he's—"

"You saved her too. I saw you dive in front of those two guys so she could get away. Don't forget all the stuff you've done." Stan looked earnestly at her as though he was proud of her sacrifice. She wasn't. She'd been spared and the more time that went by the more she wished she hadn't been. Maybe being in heaven with Simpson would be better than this hell on earth.

"It won't make a difference when I go down there. I'm sure they've already gotten word about Simpson too. They're probably beside themselves. I know I didn't tell you this, but Simpson and Alma, they liked each other. She's had a crush on him for years. He told me just that night he liked her back. She must be a wreck. Tomorrow, maybe tomorrow, I'll go down there if I can sneak away."

"You can't," Stan whispered with sharp pain in his eyes. "They aren't there. They left."

"What do you mean they left? Where would they go?" Betty felt a vice closing on her heart.

"I went this morning to check on them. I wanted to tell them you were all right, in case they hadn't heard, and break the news about Simpson if it hadn't made its way to them. When I got there the place was empty. One of the neighbors told me they left in the middle of the night, and they weren't coming back. Not ever." Stan drew in a deep breath, readying himself for Betty's reaction to the bad news he was dumping on her.

"No, you're wrong. You probably went to the wrong house or something. They wouldn't leave. Winnie promised me I'd always have a place to go, no matter what. Alma swore we'd be best friends for the rest of our lives. They wouldn't leave me. They wouldn't just leave me here all alone." Betty shook her head adamantly. She felt the urge to strike out at Stan who was timidly moving closer to her.

"They did. They're gone. But they left this note for you. The neighbor asked me to make sure you got it." Stan pulled a folded piece of paper out of his pocket and tried to hand it to Betty.

"I don't want that," she barked, slapping his hand away so hard it stung her palm. "I don't want a letter from them. I don't want an explanation. I want—I want—" Betty folded over onto herself and began to sob. "I want to go with them. I want to be wherever they are. One night and I'm alone again."

"You're not alone. I'm here. I'll be your friend. I promise. This isn't over. I'm not going sit around and do nothing. Edenville is going to change. I'm going to make it change." Stan slammed his fist into his hand, and Betty jumped at the edge in his voice.

"Don't you get it, that's why they killed him? He tried to do what's right and they murdered him. You want to end up the same way?" Betty stared at him through tear-blurred eyes and waited for him to agree with her.

"The only thing in the world I want is to have my brother back, but if I can't, I'll be damned if I let him die for nothing. People are going to know my name. They're going to listen to me. You can help me; we can do it together." Stan stepped forward again and looked oddly hopeful.

"Are you crazy?" she asked in breathy exasperation. "How do you suppose we go about that?"

"What they did, the people they killed, that can't be swept under the rug. People in town are disgusted by it. They're fed up with being afraid of the Klan. There's a minister from Arkansas who's coming here next week. He's bringing a large group with him."

"So what? They've done that in other parts of the country, and it's just more bloodbath." Betty wanted to slap Stan across the face just in hopes of getting reality to sink in to him again.

"He's white. The people coming with him are white. They've made a difference in other parts of the country. The media follows them. They have the numbers. I want to be a part of that." Stan's face was crimson with a fierce determination.

"It's not going to bring Simpson back. You know that, right? Nothing we do will bring him back." Betty's voice was soft not wanting to deliver the blow that could break his fragile heart.

"I know," Stan conceded staring down at his shoes. "And reading this note won't make your friends being gone any less real. I'm sorry they left you. But at least you get a little piece of them to say goodbye to. I wish I had that from Simpson."

Betty grabbed the paper Stan shoved toward her again. When she unfolded it, some pressed flower petals dropped out. She recognized them instantly as the flowers she'd brought to Winnie earlier that week. The ones that had managed to survive in the snow.

My dearest sweet Betty,

I know I've broken my promise to you, and I'm eternally sorry. There is nothing I can say right now that will mend the fractures in your heart. And worse than that, I know our leaving has made your sorrow even deeper. I'll never forgive myself for that even if someday you do. To leave you in a time like this was an impossible choice but one I had to make.

Please know if you feel alone it's not true. Our love will be with you everywhere you go and in everything you do. Hold us as close as you will Simpson's memory for both were forged in the deepest love.

You will survive this, Betty. It won't be easy. Right now you're in the middle of the kind of heartbreak that is bone deep. It will come in waves and you'll want to drown in it. You'll promise yourself you won't cry, and then you'll break that promise a million times. But someday it will change. Your heart will begin to see vibrant colors again. Because grief is not a place to stay, it's a doorway to pass through.

I don't have the words to make you feel better. And I don't have arms that can reach you. But I have a heart that will always hold a place for you. And I hope there is a place in yours for us. There might be days it feels too painful to remember what we all shared, but I hope you realize the love we have is too amazing to forget.

I saw you throw yourself down to save me. That image will be seared in my mind for the remainder of my life. There will never be a day we don't think of you and speak your name in our house wherever that ends up being.

If the world is ever different, if the grace of God allows, we will see each other again someday. Until then find a way to rise above. Remember everything I ever taught you, because I will remember all you've taught me.

With the deepest love,

Your family—Winnie, Nate, and Alma.

Chapter Twenty-Two

Betty hadn't felt like she was ready to change the world. Surely she hadn't been prepared to do so. But ironically, not being able to hear Winnie's voice anymore made the words she'd spoken in the past resound powerfully in Betty's mind. She was far more equipped for battle than she realized.

When taking up a picket sign felt terrifying, she remembered Winnie saying it doesn't matter what you say you'd do, it only matters what you actually get up and do. So she got up and did it. As did Stan. When it was time to sit out all night on the cold concrete with hundreds of other students who were willing to face the Klan, she remembered Winnie telling her change never came from a comfortable place. When she was spat on, shoved, threatened, and afraid, she remembered it was hate causing all this pain, and throughout history hate had yet to win.

On the days she wasn't sure she could go on fighting for what she believed, a whisper would pass across her ear, letting her knew she wasn't alone. The changes did come. The world did start to see. Not all at once. Not without more violence. But a drop in the ocean still adds water.

"Rumor has it the FBI has rounded up two hundred Klan members in Mississippi. That's where my family went. I wonder if any of them were arrested," Stan said as he poured Betty another glass of sweet tea.

"I heard they're labeling them as terrorists now. It's about time," Betty agreed, passing the newspaper across the table to him. "Have you heard anything from your family since they left?"

"Not a word. I doubt I ever will. If the Jeffrey family here hadn't taken me in, I don't know where I'd be. But I sure as hell wasn't going with them." Stan and Betty spent most afternoons sitting out on the porch of the family who'd been kind enough to let Stan stay with them so he could finish high school in Edenville. The less time she spent at home the better. Her father's power in the world was evaporating while hers was growing stronger. That tipped the scales to an uncomfortable level and made their already awkward house even more so. Staying away was the best she could do.

"I'm glad you didn't go." Betty smiled. "Going on without you would have been impossible."

"You're making me blush," he joked as he rolled his eyes. "There was no chance I was leaving you. No chance I ever will. Have you given any thought to what you'll be doing after you graduate next week? I know you've heard from a couple colleges, but you never told me your plans."

"I've been waiting." Betty shrugged and gave a coy smile.

"Waiting for what? To break my heart?" Stan asked, protectively covering his chest with his hands.

"For you to give me a reason to stay." Betty laughed.

* * * *

"Wait—wait—wait . . ."

Jules waved her hands frantically, sending Frankie shooting up off her mother's lap. "This is too much. I can't even . . ." Jules glared at her mother as though she were trying to ensure she was telling the truth.

166

"Are we hearing this right?" Bobby asked scratching his head. "Are you saying that Stan, your first husband and Jules's dad, is the boy you're talking about in your story? He's Simpson's brother? That's how you fell in love?"

"Yes," Betty said simply. She'd anticipated this revelation would be met with shock and suspected Jules may be feeling even a bit angry.

Jules's mouth was wide open as she tried to process the information coming her way. "Ma, I'm in my thirties. How in the world did I not know my father was one of eight boys? How did I not know his brother was killed right here in town. How could you keep this story from me?" There was a nip of annoyance in her voice.

"Your father didn't consider those people his family, therefore they weren't your family. They all moved out of Edenville and never looked back. As for Simpson, that story has more layers than can be summed up so quickly. I was always afraid to peel back any of it for fear of spilling it all out." Betty swallowed back the urge to tell Jules it felt impossible before this moment to even speak their names.

"He was my uncle. His blood spilled right here, somewhere I probably walk on a regular basis, and you couldn't even tell me?" Jules looked to Michael for backup, but he stayed quiet.

"This was one of the darkest moments of my life that happened in a place and with people I've remained around to this day. I walk by those memories all the time. I look people in the eye every day who lived that story with me. It's my cross to bear, please don't tell me how I should have carried it." Betty felt her cheeks burning but

167

beat back her growing frustration as she tried to see her daughter's point.

"I've grown up my whole life hearing next to nothing about any of my extended family. I don't know much about your parents. I don't know a thing about my father's family. I feel like you've been hiding it from me for all these years. I could have helped you. I could have listened a long time ago."

"That's good, dear, but I couldn't have talked about it a long time ago. I'm sorry you've lived without knowing any of this or anything about your roots. That wasn't fair of me, but know that my reasons for keeping it from you weren't malicious. It was self-preservation. I just couldn't," Betty said fighting a rush of emotion.

Jules rushed toward her looking instantly apologetic. "No I'm sorry, Ma. I'm being stupid. It's just so much to take in. I'm sitting listening to your story, crying about this boy who died a hero and then to hear he's my father's brother just hit me hard. I have so many questions. Is this why Daddy became a police officer? Did you ever see Winnie, Nate, or Alma again?"

"Well there is a bit more to the story," Betty admitted as she glanced around the porch to see if everyone was still interested. Judging by their expressions, they certainly were.

"You obviously reconnected with them since you've been in contact through the letters," Michael deduced, looking completely intrigued.

"That's where the story gets interesting." Betty grinned.

"How could it possibly get any more interesting?" Frankie asked, shaking her head in disbelief.

"Wait, I need to know more," Jules begged, touching her mother's hand gently. "Can you answer some questions for me?"

"Of course. I think I owe you at least that." Betty tucked her daughter's hair back and caressed her cheek.

"Your parents. They died when I was little. I don't remember them. Did anything change? Did you make peace with them?" It broke Betty's heart to watch her daughter reeling from the truth of the past. Like always Betty felt it her job to ease the pain in her daughter's heart. Luckily she had a bit of something to do it with.

"My mother died very suddenly of an aneurysm. It came as a shock, and sadly, she and I never really had a chance to connect the way I'd hoped. When you were born she was happy; she was a good grandmother to you. It's important you know that. She rocked you and sang to you. She loved you deeply. She loved me too. But sometimes the only way to go on is to accept the apology you never get. That's how I got to a place with my mother that I could be with my mother and not feel angry." Betty hoped that Jules, who normally didn't suffer fools, would be able to accept this. It became clear she couldn't.

"How can that be? How could she not be proud of you, or if she was, how could she be such a coward she couldn't tell you? I can't believe I'm descended from this woman. I can't believe you are. If she were here now I'd give her a piece of my mind," Jules roared as she clenched her hands into fists.

"Child, like I've been saying since you were a toddler, I appreciate your zeal, but your little head is gonna pop off your shoulders if you don't calm down. My mother was flawed, but so am I, and so are you.

Maybe all in different ways but it's unavoidable. My mother loved me. I know that for sure even if she couldn't tell me. I don't hold a grudge about it."

"I do," Jules snipped but quieted when Betty nodded over to Frankie who was watching this unfold like a television drama. "Maybe we should talk about it later."

"I think Grammy's right," Frankie interjected. "Things were different back then, and I'm glad she's not my mama, but she's still a part of our family. I forgive her."

"I'm taking credit for that part of you," Michael joked and everyone but Jules snickered. "This is a lot of information Jules. I'm not saying it's easy but what's done is done."

Jules rolled her eyes and shook her head in frustration. "Excuse me for being bothered that my roots are made of what I view as despicable people."

Piper, always one to try to cut the tension jumped in. "I'm sure most people can look back on their family tree and find one unhappy surprise or another. What's really important is what came out of that. You should be very proud of your mother. I know I am."

"Thank you dear, but I did hardly anything compared to what some did. People were severely injured or killed, protesting and marching," Betty said, shooing away all the admiration. It wasn't the point of the story, and she didn't want everyone to get lost in that.

"What about your dad?" Jules asked, her face still twisted up in anger. She was looking for someone to blame.

"When I married your father he didn't come. He didn't walk me down the aisle, and he didn't shake Stan's hand. When we bought our first house, he didn't come see it. He never stepped foot in it actually. We never discussed anything besides the weather and other pointless things." Before Betty could continue Jules cut in.

"Bastard," she muttered and then covered her mouth quickly and looked down at her daughter.

"Mommy, don't say curse words," Frankie scolded.

"At least let me finish," Betty insisted and gestured for Jules to go sit back down. "On the day you were born I didn't expect to see him in the hospital. He'd stayed away from every big moment in my life before that so why should this be any different? By this time the Klan had disbanded, and civil rights had spread far and wide, making huge changes in the world. I no longer needed his validation. I'd found happiness without him.

"You were a pain in the ass even back then, and after delivering you I needed some rest. While you were in the nursery I fell asleep. A little while later I woke up, and my daddy was sitting in the chair next to my bed. He told me everyone else had gone down to look at the baby. He looked so uncomfortable sitting there alone with me. I felt bad for him. I was still a little groggy, and I think he could see that. Maybe that's why he took the opportunity to actually talk to me."

"What did he say?" Jules asked, looking like she'd already written him off as an unredeemable waste of space.

"I remember him fiddling around with a pocket watch he had. It had been chained in his pocket since my first memories of him. He pulled it out and let it spin around until it settled and dangled in front of his face. He told me his daddy had given it to him, and his daddy before him had handed it down too. It was a piece of our family. He laughed when he told me he wished I were a boy, because he always imaged handing this watch down to his son. Now since I had a girl too, he'd have to wait for a grandson to hand it to. I actually apologized, though I think it was just the fog of exhaustion speaking.

He went quiet for a few moments before swallowing hard. I'll never forget the look in his eyes as he spoke. It was the most honest I'd ever seen him. With shaking hands he tucked the watch away and told me he got a lot more handed down to him from his dad and his grandfather. His beliefs, his temper, and his hood were all things he thought he'd hand down some day too. If he'd had a boy, surely he would have."

"So you're sitting there, you've just delivered me, and he's blaming you for not being a boy and for not having a boy?" Jules looked at Michael for support, but he just rubbed her shoulder and encouraged her to keep listening.

"So my daddy went on, staring at the ceiling while he spoke. It's a good thing, he said as he nodded his head, that I'd been a girl. Maybe it was time to stop handing some of this stuff down. Maybe it was better that way. With that he stood and left. I closed my eyes, smiled, and went back to sleep." Betty watched as everyone on the porch seemed to soften a bit. That was what she was hoping for. She'd come a long way in putting her past behind her; she wasn't trying to make everyone upset about it.

"I guess that's something," Jules conceded.

"How did he die?" Bobby asked, his inquisitive police brain always churning through the details.

"Pneumonia, after a bout of the flu," Betty explained. "I sat with him in the hospital for four days, watching his chest rise and fall with labored breaths. He was in and out of consciousness. The poor guy, I finally had him trapped." Betty let out a breathy laugh though she was alone in it.

"What do you mean?" Clay asked, leaning forward to see his wife's face.

"I mean he couldn't go anywhere. He just had to sit there and listen to me talk about how I forgave him, how much I loved him, and I was sorry."

"What were you sorry for?" Frankie asked, eyeing her grandmother skeptically.

"If I forgot about everything else happening in the world, if I didn't take right and wrong into the equation, I still disappointed my father. I still hurt him over the years. I couldn't be the child he hoped for, and a part of me was sorry for that. If I didn't take my opportunity to tell him, I'd still be living with the burden of that today."

"Did he say anything back?" Frankie asked, clearly hoping he had, and this would be the happy ending of a perfectly scripted movie.

"No," Betty admitted, dropping her head down. "But one of the last things he did with the little strength he had was hand me his pocket watch. I know he was telling me to give it new meaning, to hand it down to a whole different generation of people."

"Wow," Michael breathed as he leaned back in his chair and stretched his back. "That is a truly amazing story, Betty. I've always respected the woman you are, but I'll admit I'm going to have a hard time teasing you about anything now. I mean, don't get me wrong, I'll still find a way, but it'll be harder."

"I'm sure you will," Betty giggled, waving Michael off. "There's more to the story, like I said, but we don't have to finish it up tonight if everyone is tired."

"I still can't believe you did all that," Frankie cut in. "Weren't you so scared? Even jumping in front of those men to save Winnie, weren't you afraid?"

"All the time," Betty admitted.

"And you haven't told us how you reconnected with Winnie," Bobby added. "When did you and Alma start writing each other? I'm surprised you've never talked about her before; we never had the chance to meet her."

"You sure you want to hear all this? It's getting late." Betty had seen yawns beginning to become contagious a few minutes ago, and she didn't want anyone feeling trapped here.

"We want to hear it, all of it. What was in her last letter to you?" Piper asked, remembering the envelope Betty seemed reluctant to open.

"I haven't brought myself to reading it yet," Betty admitted, pulling the envelope off the table next to her rocking chair. "In the last letter she sent me she told me there would only be one more, and when I got it I'd know she'd passed on. Reading it would signify the end of everything we've ever had."

"Read it now," Clay suggested as he rubbed Betty's back supportively. "We're all here with you. We all know who she was now. Let us share it with you."

As Betty thought it over the pitch black driveway was burst open by the bright beams of headlights.

"Who could that be?" Bobby asked, getting to his feet quickly. Michael followed suit and strained his eyes to try to identify the car.

174

"It's a cab," Michael said, looking over his shoulder at Betty as if she might know something the rest of them didn't. But she shot back a puzzled look that seemed to put everyone on edge. History had told them, as the consummate puppetmaster of all things, if Betty didn't know what was going on, they should all be worried.

"I think I should have read that letter," Betty laughed as she stood, having to brace herself against the railing of the porch. Every eye bounced from her to the person stepping out of the cab then back just in time to see her giant smile.

Chapter Twenty-Three

"Ma, who is that?" Jules asked, walking beside Betty as she stepped down the stairs.

"Betty?" the man asked as the cab driver pulled his bag from the trunk, and he slung it over his shoulder. His hair was salt and pepper and the wrinkles at the side of his eyes had grown deeper, but he was still the way she remembered him.

"What are doing here?" Betty asked, racing down the stairs with a skip in her step she hadn't felt in decades.

"You didn't read the letter, did you?" he asked, tossing his head back with a laugh. "I've been traveling for the last twenty-seven hours to get here, and I should have known you would have held that letter and not read it."

Betty flashed the envelope she had in her hand and they chuckled at the irony. "I was just sitting out here with all my family telling them our story. Well, most of it. I suppose with you being here I'll have to keep them up late tonight and finish what I started."

"Ma, I don't want to be rude, but who is this?" Jules asked, looking confused and a bit concerned.

"Can't you see it dear? Look at him in the light," Betty insisted as she dragged him up the stairs under the light of the porch for everyone to see.

Bobby was the first notice it. Maybe it was his keen police officer's eye. "He looks just like Stan. He looks like your dad, Jules, but with dark hair."

"Oh my gosh," Jules said in astonishment as she tilted her head to see him from different angles. "Who?" she asked her mother as the tears began to form in her eyes.

"This is your uncle," Betty announced as she slipped her arm into his. "This is Simpson."

"But, how?" Frankie asked, jumping to her feet. "He was killed, wasn't he? You said they killed him that night. Did he come back from the dead?"

"Well, for four hundred thirty-one days I thought they had killed him. Then I got a second letter from Winnie, and everything changed." Betty squeezed his arm, unable to believe he was back in Edenville, a place he swore he would never return to. "I never expected to see you back here."

"I don't understand," Jules said, covering her mouth in astonishment. "What are you doing here?"

"I better read this," Betty said, flashing the envelope again.

"Out loud," Michael insisted, clearly trying to piece it all together.

Dear Betty,

As I told you this will be my last letter. I won't draw out my goodbye. There is nothing to say here that hasn't already been said. It's written on both our hearts. So the only thing I'll ask of you is the biggest favor of all. I give back to you the one thing you gave to me all those years ago.

Please carry him through this time the way your love has always carried me. The only reason I can close my eyes and leave this earth is because I know he will not be alone. The stories of the family you have built remind me so much of my mother, and I know she would be so proud of you. Add my dearest Simpson to your treasured family.

Love always,

Alma

"What the hell is going on?" Frankie asked, tossing her hands up in the air in complete frustration.

"Language," multiple adults on the porch shouted at once, and Frankie shrank back. But her exasperation was certainly being felt by most of them.

"What do you need Simpson, a drink? Are you hungry? I can fix you a plate. You must have had quite the journey to get back here." Betty led him to a chair that he gladly took.

"I might not make it off this porch if you don't tell them the rest of your story. I think I can wait for something to eat. They don't look like they can wait to hear what happened to me." Simpson looked around the porch with that crooked smile Betty remembered so fondly.

"Popcorn," Piper said, pushing a bowl into his lap. "Now talk." She laughed, gesturing for them to get on with the story.

"Where did you leave off?" Simpson asked as he tossed a handful of popcorn into his mouth. "I guess I was dead already, judging by the way everyone is looking at me. I can assure you, I'm not a ghost."

"I hadn't gotten to the part where Winnie wrote me a second letter yet. It was just after Stan and I got engaged. It was the happiest I had been in a long time, but I was sad not to be able to share it with the people I loved the most. The day the letter came that all changed. Betty reached into her shoebox of old things and grabbed a faded greeting card covered on every available surface with writing.

Dear Betty,

I've been waiting so long for this day. We've all debated it over and over again. When would the moment be right? When could we share with you the joy we've kept secret for so long. That day is today. We heard last week that Stan and Simpson's father had died. It was one of many factors in our decision. The Klan itself is mostly depleted, and the civil rights movement is forging ahead with great victories. The fear that lived in us, that kept us from communicating, has become smaller than our desperate need to hear from you.

The first thing I must ask is for is your forgiveness. When the joy of the news I have to tell you subsides, there will undoubtedly be anger for keeping you in the dark. Under the very troubling circumstance by which this all transpired Nate and I felt it necessary to tell no one the truth of the matter. Second, I ask that you please vow to keep this a secret. There are all manners of challenges that would come if you revealed this to anyone.

I don't even know where to begin. On that horrible night after the dance, you witnessed so many things. You saw the culmination of hate, the bravery of a hero, and the test of even your own will. But what you didn't see is the murder of Simpson. That's because he was not killed. As the fighting ensued he was beaten badly, slashed, and stabbed, but he survived. After I ran home and told Nate what had happened, he charged up to the school. The police had not yet arrived, but the Klan had dispersed, as you would expect cowards to do. Nate found Simpson at the edge of a fire, about to be consumed by it. He lifted his very broken body up and carried him back to our house. We did everything we could to patch him up and then hid him. The following day we got word about who died, and Simpson's name was on the list. We heard how cold and cruel his mother had been, and we knew if he survived this it wouldn't be long before they tried again to kill him.

In that moment Nate and I decided if he were to have any chance at a real life it would need to be far from Edenville. When he was well enough to travel, we packed up our truck in the dead of the night and escaped. Simpson is alive. He is alive and well.

We've opened a special mailbox that doesn't have our address in case anyone in town still has the desire to hurt us and intercepts one of these letters. Please write back. We are so desperate to hear from you. I pray you're happy. I pray you forgive our omission of the truth, and I pray to see you again someday soon.

Your family,

Winnie, Nate, Alma, and Simpson.

There was not a composed person or dry eye on the porch as Betty closed the card and placed it back in the box. "I sobbed for hours after I got that. I cried nearly as much when I found out he was alive as I had when I thought he was dead," Betty explained.

"Did you tell Stan?" Piper asked, completely intrigued. "He was his brother and your fiancé. Did you do what Winnie asked and keep the secret, or did you tell him?"

"I told him," Betty replied incredulously. "I knew darn well if Winnie had known the circumstances, she'd have insisted I tell him. Plus the poor guy walked in on my wailing away like a loony bird, so I had to tell him I had a good reason for it."

"What happened next?" Bobby asked, shooting her a look like she was getting off track, and he wanted just the facts of it all.

"We cried together. We laughed. We got mad they didn't tell us. And we forgave them. That night we each wrote a letter and sent them to their post office box in Arizona. So started the communication that would span forty more years.

"You never went to see them?" Frankie asked with a twisted up face. "Arizona isn't that far."

"We saw them once more. Winnie had made sure she'd never step on Edenville soil again. She'd written off the entire state and most of the surrounding ones. Money was very tight all around, so getting there was harder than you think."

"I thought you'd never left Edenville," Piper said. "When I first met you and you went out to Illinois with us you said that."

"This trip never existed. My mother thought I was at a girls' campout for the weekend. We didn't buy any knick-knacks to commemorate it. It was a secret, so I've lived like it never happened. For a long time it was as if none of this ever happened."

"That's certainly the impression you get here in Edenville," Bobby groaned. "In all the years I've lived here, I've never seen any type of memorial or even the discussion of what happened."

"Dark times, Bobby," Betty said gently. "People were not all bad then, even if it sounded that way from my story. There were plenty of folks who weren't the least bit prejudiced, probably a lot of stories just like mine. The problem was there were a few terrible voices that came together very loudly. It scared people. When integration was going on people came in from other states to knock on doors and rile up people who otherwise weren't worked up at all. I don't blame the whole town, though you might feel different, Simpson; I won't speak for you."

"I'll be honest, I haven't given it much thought over the years. I've made it a point not to. When I do, it takes me somewhere I don't want to be." Simpson busied himself with a couple more handfuls of popcorn and waited for the subject to change.

"You married Alma?" Jules asked, still looking like she was staring at a ghost. "So she was my aunt? I'd have liked to see you guys. I would have gone wherever to meet her."

"I'm sure she'd have loved you," Simpson said apologetically. "We weren't in Arizona long before Winnie passed away, and I joined the service. I explained the situation to my commanding officer, and he was empathetic. Being in an interracial marriage was incredibly difficult. We knew we'd do better the farther away we could get. We took Nate with us and traveled around the world."

"Did you start a family?" Piper cut in. "If you don't mind me asking."

"We have two sons. Both in the military now too, and I couldn't be prouder of them. After I retired Alma and I stayed near my last post on an island off Japan. It was quiet, and we lived very many peaceful years there," Simpson explained. "Nate lived to be eighty, and we were happy to have him around."

"How did you and Alma start dating? I can't imagine what a whirlwind that must have been," Jules asked, finally sounding optimistic again.

Simpson opened his mouth to speak, slipped his hat off his head, and held it to his chest. When he couldn't seem to muster the words, Betty cut in.

"That's Simpson's story to tell if he ever feels like he wants to. He's been on a long journey back here, and I'm sure he's exhausted. We should let him get settled. I'll need to do some stuff up in Jules's old room to make it comfortable for you. Unless you like pink and frills?"

"I told Alma a million times I didn't want to put you out, but she made me swear I'd come out here to you. It was her dying wish, but you should know I'm not sure I'll be staying all that long. Being back here . . ." he trailed off as he drew in a deep breath.

"Well you're staying at least the night; the rest we can talk about tomorrow. I'm just so happy to have you here. Seeing you again, wrapping my arms around you, gives me so much joy," Betty squeezed his shoulder with one hand and wiped her tears away with the other.

"You remind me so much of Winnie," he smiled and patted her hand that rested on his shoulder. "Alma is right; she'd be mighty proud of you."

"I don't want this to be over," Jules admitted as she wiped a tear from her own eye. "My family just grew tonight. You're my daddy's brother. You look so much

183

like him, and I don't want to go home. I have a million questions for you about him. Please don't be too much in a rush to leave. I'd be sorry to see you go."

"Me being back here, letting people know I'm alive after all these years, will surely bring lots of turmoil. I'd hate to bring all that to kind folks. You seem like such normal people," Simpson explained, as he looked them all over. "I'd hate to put you through any drama because of me."

A low laugh broke out between all of them as Piper spoke. "With the exception of Frankie here, you'd be the only one on this porch so far not to come with trouble. And her only excuse is the fact that she's not been on the planet long enough to have stirred any up yet. We might look sweet and innocent, but we've all had our share of trouble."

"I promise I won't be running out of here too quick. I gave my word to Alma, but don't go out of your way for me. I've lived in the farthest corners of the world in all sorts of conditions; I can be happy anywhere."

"I hope that includes Edenville," Jules said, looking at him again and seeming amazed by how much he resembled her father.

"We should pile the kids into the car and get them into their own beds," Bobby suggested as he rose and pulled Piper to her feet. Everyone followed suit and started making their way toward the door. Bobby stopped in front of Simpson and extended his hand.

"I just want you to know your brother Stan was like a father to me. He was one of the most honorable men I've ever met. He's part of the reason I became a police officer."

Simpson nodded his head and shook Bobby's hand. "I've heard all about you in Betty's letters. I'm sure my brother would be glad to know you've been here looking out for Betty and Jules. I know I'm glad."

"I look forward to getting to know you better," Piper chimed in as she passed on her way into the house to retrieve the twins. Jules and Frankie laced their fingers together and stood before Simpson, not sure what they were supposed to do next. Luckily he had something to say.

He addressed Frankie with a smile. "You look so much like your grandmother Betty back when I knew her. You've got that same look in your eye."

"Which look?" Frankie asked, glancing up at her mother nervously, as though she had something wrong with her.

"The look that says you'll be the kind of person who is going to shake the world. Maybe it'll just be a gentle shake, but that's all it takes some times," Simpson assured her.

"I just don't get it. That whole story doesn't make sense to me. You all suffered. You had to stay away from each other. You didn't get to see your family, and my Grammy was so alone. It's terrible." Frankie shook her head and looked over at Betty for some advice, the way she always did in tough situations.

"The story is terrible, but our lives weren't. We found our own kinds of happiness. But the world is still far from perfect. It's your generation I'm counting on to take that hurt and pain and passion to the next level."

"How?" Frankie asked, looking utterly confused by the responsibility.

"By being exactly who you are. When you see someone in pain, stop and help them. When you see someone alone, be a friend. Know there is value to every single life. The most important lesson I ever learned was that every single group of people, divided up however they like by race, religion, or beliefs, has in it the most wonderful, kind-hearted, peaceful, and loving people that you will be happy you met, and every single group of people, divided however they like by race, religion, or beliefs, has in it the poorest excuse for humans, and you will be sorry you met them. There is no way to know by looking at someone which type they are." Betty reached out and pulled Frankie in for a hug. "It's a lot to think of when you're still small. That's why we're all here. You don't have to get it right all the time. We'll be around to help you."

"I love you, Grammy." Frankie sighed into Betty's shoulder. "I'm sorry you had to go through so much. I wish I could make that better."

"You've made it better every day you've been alive. You turned me into a Grammy. I can't tell you how much that helped me. No you go on and help your mama get the baby set to go." She kissed the crown of Frankie's head and waved them all inside. "Clay, will you take Simpson in and get him a plate while I get the room upstairs settled for him?"

Clay stood and kissed Betty on the cheek. "You find ways to impress me more every day. Come on Simpson; let's get you something to eat."

"I've heard a lot about your restaurant, Clay. I'm looking forward to eating there," Simpson complimented, but he stopped short when Clay waived him off.

"It's Betty's place really. She's just kind enough to let me cook there sometimes. She's brilliant with food, and now I know why."

The men disappeared through the screen door of the house, and Betty began to follow, but Michael caught her arm.

"Hold up," he said, and she turned to face him. "The lawyer in me has a million questions about the legal side of what happened to Simpson: whether anyone was brought to justice for the murders. I'll go find those answers on my own rather than dragging anyone through that."

"But?" Betty asked, raising a knowing eyebrow at her son-in-law. She could read him like a book, and he had a tricky look in his eyes.

"I saw that letter as you were reading it. Maybe no one else noticed but it was far longer than you read. Is there any reason you stopped short? Anything else we should know about Simpson being back here?"

"Damn you, Michael Cooper, and your impeccable vision and inquisitive nature. We're going to have our hands full if Frankie has inherited that from you. Yes, the letter was much longer."

"It's your personal letter; you have no obligation to share with any of us if you don't want to. I'm just saying if there is anything in there that means trouble, you know you can tell me. If there is more to the story, you can share it with me." He looked down at her affectionately, and she felt so lucky to have had him marry into the family.

Betty pulled the letter from her pocket and handed it over. "Is anything ever uncomplicated with us? Why should we start now? Just don't get all worked up about it, okay?"

"Do I ever get worked up about anything?" Michael challenged with a mischievous smile.

"No you don't, and thank goodness for that because I'm not sure what I'd do if you and Jules both were hotheads." With a laugh she headed toward the screen door. "I wouldn't give that letter to anyone else; you should know that. She mentions you in the letter, but don't let it go to your head."

Michael nodded and chuckled as he unfolded the paper and skimmed to catch up to the part Betty hadn't read. Sitting alone on the porch he tried to understand why Betty had withheld this from the group.

With Simpson being alone now I know old ghosts that we've fought to keep at bay will surface again. When I left Edenville I left with the people who loved me. When he left, all he had with him was the knowledge that his own family wanted him dead. The physical toll that beating took on him eventually healed, but the heartbreak is still there. He's covered it over with our love, but I'm afraid of what will happen when I'm gone. If he stays here on this quiet island, he will surely go mad. Even now, the less able I am to be with him the more I hear the nightmares consume him in his sleep.

I truly believe he must face this. I don't know the legal ramifications that might await him. Perhaps if Michael is as brilliant a lawyer as you always go on about, he can help with that. He's lived under an alias so long, and I don't want him to get in any trouble, but he must face his past. He must go back to Edenville and heal once I'm gone. If he doesn't you'll lose us both, and I don't want that to happen.

Help him navigate the transition back to being Simpson. Help him face the sorrow of not only losing me but of all that's happened to him. Remind him of the fun we all had and the love we all shared.

I'd be lying if I said it would be easy. He never speaks about the past. But you have this annoying quality of getting people to open up, and I implore you to use it on him. It was a promise to me that's brought him there, but it'll be up to you to keep him long enough to change anything in his heart.

There are a lot of ways you can love someone. Simpson is my best friend, my husband, the father of my children, and he takes up the largest place in my heart. But you, Betty, were the great love of my life. I'm counting on you. Simpson saved my mother's life, and now he needs saving.

Michael sat for a moment as he folded the letter and held it tight in his hand. He could hear the bustle of everyone packing up in the house and saying goodbye. The enormity of what Alma was asking of Betty was hard to wrap his head around. The legal side of what had happened could be figured out, he assumed, but the task of fixing someone's broken heart was a tall order. Before he could let that worry overwhelm him Betty stepped back outside.

"Quite a job I have ahead of me," Betty sighed as she tossed her dish towel over her shoulder.

"Good thing you've got an extensive amount of experience in the field of fixing everyone," Michael reassured her.

"The problem is I've barely gotten my own heart fixed on some of these matters. This is the first time I've talked about it in so long. I may not be up to the task of helping him at all," Betty confessed as she put her hand up to her aching forehead.

"I guess you better get your gardening gloves on then," Michael instructed as Betty twisted her face in confusion. "You've got some more flowers to grow, and the ground is ready for snow. It'll be difficult but with you Betty, nothing is impossible."

The End of Flowers in the Snow

Continue the story in Book 2, Kiss in the Wind

Are you curious about how Betty's modern day family came to be? You can read how it all began in Chasing Justice Book 1 of The Piper Anderson Series. Download your FREE copy today.

My Great-Grandfather(Pep), My Mother & Aunt in 1963, witnessing flowers in the snow.

Author Contact:
Website: AuthorDanielleStewart.com
Email: AuthorDanielleStewart@Gmail.com
Facebook: Author Danielle Stewart
Twitter: @DStewartAuthor

Books by Danielle Stewart

Piper Anderson Series
Book 1: Chasing Justice
Book 2: Cutting Ties
Book 3: Changing Fate
Book 4: Finding Freedom
Book 5: Settling Scores
Book 6: Battling Destiny
Book 7: Chris & Sydney Collection – Choosing
Christmas & Saving Love

Piper Anderson Extras:
Betty's Journal - Bonus Material(suggested to be read
after Book 4 to avoid spoilers)

Edenville Series – A Piper Anderson Spin Off:
Book 1: Flowers in the Snow
Book 2: Kiss in the Wind
Book 3: Stars in a Bottle

The Clover Series:
Hearts of Clover - Novella & Book 2: (Half My Heart &
Change My Heart)
Book 3: All My Heart
Book 4: Facing Home

The Rough Waters Series:
Book 1: The Goodbye Storm
Book 2: The Runaway Storm
Book 3: The Rising Storm

Midnight Magic Series:
Amelia

The Barrington Billionaire Series:
Book 1: Fierce Love
Book 2: Wild Eyes

62472132R00120

Made in the USA
Lexington, KY
07 April 2017